The Christmas Chiave

The Christmas Chiave

A Boston Novella

J.P. Polidoro

To order additional copies of this book, contact:
Xlibris Corporation
1-888-795-4274
www.Xlibris.com
Orders@Xlibris.com
48713

Dedication

For my children and grandchildren
May they always seek, and hold 'the Key' to Christmas

Chapter 1

The near Christmas snow fell in large flakes on this one particular winter's day. It fell on Hanover Street in Boston's Little Italy, the *North End.* Omnipresent were the smells of Italian food and pastries, a ubiquitous combination of opposing aromas that were not unappealing but still synergistic. Garlic, tomato sauce, basil, anise, almond and lemon permeated the neighborhood from block to block.

The quiet air was serene and the lampposts exuded an aura of a traditional story-of-old. Street lamps lit in darkness were individually haloed as the flakes gathered in the air to form temporary doilies of white art that encompassed each globe. They seemed to merge and cling to one another in midair, then spin and roll gently making the flakes even bigger than one could imagine they could be. Children watched from upper floor apartment windows. It was early evening and their black silhouettes were peering through window curtains of lace that were held back by their young hands of soft, youthful skin. They were stoic and unmoving like art and sculpture in a window frame, occasionally shifting to justify the fact that they were children and not dolls.

A cab pulled up to the frozen curb on the corner of Hanover and Cross Streets. The tires squeaked rhythmically on the cold snow as the car slowed and eventually stopped. The passenger had directed the cabbie to stop just short of Mother Anna's Restaurant. I was the person who asked him to stop at the beginning of the street, the one closest to Route 93 and a famed Italian market and wine and cheese shop. The white cab, not yellow, had black lettering on the doors that read Emerald Cab Company and the logo of a shamrock in green seemed ironic in a historic Italian neighborhood.

Perhaps it was an uncanny protest in silence since the North End in the early 1800s was the home of Irish immigrants. Many were poor and desolate and living in squalor in run-down boarding houses. By 1850, one half of the residents in the North End were of Irish descent. One million of the Irish immigrated to America over a forty-year period of 1815 to 1855. The Portuguese and other ethnicities, including the Italians, would also settle there and fish from the local ports and beyond Boston Harbor. Fish were plentiful then, especially beyond the Isles in cold deep water.

"Right here is fine, Sir," I instructed him, in a voice that quivered from anxiety. I wanted the North End to be the same, the same as I had remembered it years earlier. The cabbie stopped and totaled the fare. Snow piled up on the corners of the windshield. He said little as the wipers tried to combat the large flakes that desired to obstruct his view.

I owed him $15.50 for the ride from a downtown hotel. Much of the cab bill was accrued and accumulated from sitting in traffic near the Boston Common and around Tremont Street. The rest of the bill was merely the fee at each ¼ mile, an exorbitant expectation for travel around Bean Town in the modern world. Taking a cab was a trade off from parking in public garages. Neither was cheap.

"Your change from the twenty," grunted the cab driver. I took three dollars and tipped him but had wished I had kept the money for myself. He was no conversationalist or even courteous during the ride, and basically appeared to hate his job or perhaps the hours that he worked. The days were long and he seemed tired.

"Have a good evening," I offered to the animated, dissociated mannequin. I remember a grunt or a snide comment or two from him before I shut the door and he drove hastily and carelessly east on Hanover. Another fare was needed. It was a game of numbers and dispatchers were persistent in keeping cabs full from one ride to the next. He never even said goodbye.

I stood for a moment on the sidewalk, my shoes in deep snow and slowly rotated my head and then body, absorbing the smells and sights of the famed historic section of Boston. It was the Old Boston and the first real settlement.

For a moment, I almost remembered my youth; a youth where I had grown up in this neighborhood of Italians and Italian-American descendants from my native region of Calabria.

I was born and bred in the North End two to three blocks from where I was standing. My father had once told me as a young boy that 'one always goes home.' In my tender young years, I wasn't sure what he meant by the phrase. I sensed his presence as I looked down the street at all too familiar sights. Having been away for decades and much older in age now, I could see that he was right . . . I was home, a bit late and after his passing, but I was home. Breathing deeply and exhaling a cold smoke-like breath of steam, I began a slow journey down Hanover looking systematically and deliberately in every windowpane. They had not really changed in architecture since my recollection of them as a child. Names had changed perhaps, but not the structures. There were the restaurants with menus and plastic flowers in the windows and shops that sold 'Italian Importing' goods. The bakeries were the same, Mike's and the Modern in direct opposition to themselves, competitors to this day. I smiled as I reminisced.

I had an appointment with a Realtor named Elena LaFauci. She was the offspring of a number of LaFauci generations, the most recent of which had owned a nearby market. Although in the North End, the market faced the Faneuil Hall and Old State House complex a quarter of a mile west. We were scheduled to meet in the early evening and I rechecked the newspaper listing for her telephone number, which I had folded in quarters from the Boston Globe classified section of the paper. I still had a few minutes before heading to Prince Street, my ultimate destination. It was only two or three streets ahead on the left but I wished the journey to be longer. I needed to absorb all the sights and architecture. *Did I really grow up here? Was I really the son of a single father, by default? Did I play stickball with Aldo Spinelli and Dominick Russo on a side street when I was eight-years-of-age? Where were they today? Alive? Dead?* I had the desire to know.

My name is Giovanni 'John' Perri, often called 'Johnnie' by my peers and childhood friends and I was *home* after decades of being away.

Chapter 2

My travels had taken me to Boston for a writer's conference, the annual Independent Wordsmith Conference of New England; a gathering of authors and publishers that met in major cities around the country once a year. This year it was in Boston. Last year it was in Providence. The attendance was usually a few thousand unknown, independent authors seeking publishers, and *visa versa*, independent publishers seeking authors or their attempts on paper to pen the infamous, *Great American Novel* manuscript. It's a transient business with ebbs and tides and publishers sought out the *unknown writer(s)* who would be the next J.D. Salinger, Grace Metalious or Margaret Mitchell by serendipity, both man or woman. The independent authors are capable writers and often self-publish in order to get noticed by the 'big boys' like Random House and Doubleday or Viking that normally don't care for the 'unknown aspirants of the written word,' either fictional or historical writers. The rate of success was less than 1% it seemed and authors were criticized and shunned if the plot didn't take off in the first 25-50 pages. Children's book authors seemed to always do well . . . the market was there and lucrative.

The weeklong conference allowed ample time for the participants at the show to enjoy the noted Boston sights, perhaps to inspire more writing. For me, it was to seek my roots and revisit my youth in a familiar setting, the North End. If there were something to pen afterwards, I would know in minutes. My mind worked fast, both in writing exposé and dialogue.

While many attendees took well-deserved breaks in order to see historic sites in town and along the Freedom Trail, I had only one mission in mind—I was to return to my family home just as I had promised my father prior to his death just two months earlier. He lived his remaining years in another small town in Western Massachusetts. His long life ended from natural causes and he was a native of Boston. He claimed that his 91-years of healthy living could be attributed to a glass of red wine, a garlic clove and the occasional raw onion. One way or another, those supplements were known to lower cholesterol or augment heart function in a very positive way. Even red wine in moderation was therapeutic, so he made lots of Chianti himself. Father omitted the fact that he smoked stogies, a nasty smelling twisted cigar, or drank Grappa to excess on occasion. He omitted the lack of exercise that normally augments many diseases and kills many people these days. He had good genes, that's all!

*   *   *

The short walk to Prince Street was more of a shuffle as I absorbed the culture and scenery. I kicked the snow as I traveled along and wiped the rapid accumulation off the wrought iron fences that lined one or two properties along the pleasant journey back in time. I was acting like a kid and I had no gloves for protection. My hands remained mostly in my pockets for warmth. Holiday strings of lights, red and white and green, were strung along some of the lampposts; it made the silent street authentic Italian and festival-like. I only passed three other people or residents as I walked. No one looked familiar. Why would they? Rational people were inside and warm, shunning the snow and cold. One or two merchants were out shoveling their storefront sidewalks to encourage customers, but no one was shopping. The large flakes accumulated again as fast as they shoveled.

Prince Street, on the left, ran *north* toward Commercial, a street that passed along the wharves of Boston Harbor. Prince also ran *east* toward the Paul Revere House, perhaps the oldest home in the entire city of Boston. Halfway down Prince, I noticed a dim light over a doorway of a brick building. The steps were granite and an ornate, metal railing and fence lined both sides of the three steps. The fence looked to be protecting a garden where flowers might bloom in summer. I couldn't remember any garden.

To the right of the steps and on the first floor was a window with a common hardware store sign displayed in it:

For Sale or Rent.

A local phone number followed the posting.

Below the English words was the same message but written in Italian. The sign was really in reference to a rental or sale on the second level. The front wooden door facing the street was also carved and had old glass windows in the upper quadrants of the Christian door. The glass in each panel was wavy. The door was solid oak and the door handle made of old forged brass. I grasped the metal as if it were yesterday, the yesterdays of my youth. The door upstairs to the 'Realtor listing' was slightly ajar and beckoned me to climb the thirteen steps to the second floor. A strip of inexpensive carpet, a runner, was tacked to each step and ran contiguously up to the second level. The building itself was only two floors. The carpet was nondescript in color, especially in the dim illumination of the hallway light fixture. If the bulb at the top of the stairs was 60 watts, I think that would be 'a stretch.' I could see a coat rack on the wall as I ascended the steps to the top. The rack was old and artistically aesthetic, and possibly the same one that I remembered from years past.

I could hear the heels of a woman's shoes and she peered out of the doorway of the condo and down the stairs toward me. I was halfway up the climb when she spoke.

"Mr. Perri? Is that you?"

"Yes," I replied, courteously but somewhat apprehensive of the impending room I was about to enter.

"Hi. I'm John."

"Please come up," she enticed me, extending her arm to shake hands. I stood in the doorway briefly and went silent for the moment.

"Thank you," I responded, coyly. "How do you do. A pleasure to meet you." The nervousness dissipated as quickly as it had come.

"I'm Elena LaFauci with the residential group of Harbor Realty," she said, with a slight Italian accent. She obviously was fluent in both languages. She stood professionally stoic and was well dressed in a pantsuit as I thanked her for showing up on such a snowy and difficult night to try and negotiate Boston. It was tough to do even when the weather was nice!

"Did you have any trouble finding No. 76 Prince?" she asked.

"No, not at all, Ma'am," I replied, candidly.

She was unaware that I was knowledgeable about the North End and the local streets off of Hanover. "I found it easily, thanks."

"Feel free to wander," she encouraged me. "The rooms are quite large for a North End property. Someone must have been thinking 'children' when they made this place." I smiled at her comment and agreed. I walked into what was my parent's room and stared at the small bed that now occupied the larger bedroom. A closet stood to the right of the nightstand and I opened and closed it slowly. Above the bed was a wooden crucifix. It was plain in appearance but relevant to the décor of the apartment, now condo. The owners seemed religious as noted by the accessories. Elena watched me as I strolled slowly from room to room.

"Here's the listing sheet," she offered. I thanked her and skimmed the paper while walking from one room to another.

The kitchen seemed smaller than I remembered. I could hear her high heels clicking on the kitchen floor. It had a cadence to the sound.

The appliances in the kitchen were more modern than I would have remembered. Our appliances were GE back when. Today, they were Maytag brand and good quality.

Elena walked slowly keeping her hands behind her in a nonchalant manner; appearing to be non-obtrusive but cordial should I have questions for her.

The living room looked down on Prince and I could envision the Christmas lights that once graced the lampposts on the side streets. They were there in my mind. I asked if we could shut off the lights in the living room. She looked perplexed and threatened. I eased her mind stating that I wanted to see the streetlamps glow, and the gentle snow falling silently on the sidewalks and road below. I wanted to stand there and revisit my youth when I would peer out of the lower panes as a child and watch the clean white flakes cover the dingy roads below or hide the paper litter and occasional empty, brown bottle from some indigent or reveler of the past.

Elena respected my wishes and flipped the light switch off. She must have found me odd in my request. No one had ever asked her to dim any lights during a showing of a home before, I'm sure. She somehow knew that the vision I was transfixed upon *meant* something to me.

"You have been here before haven't you," she stated, raising an eyebrow and approaching my back. I nodded, yes. "I could sense it when you entered. Has another Realtor shown you this listing?"

"No," I replied turning around. We were now face to face.

"Do you know someone who lived here?" she inquired, walking a step or two toward the kitchen. I had not budged and I did not immediately answer her.

She heard me sigh out loud.

"I'm sorry," she added, embarrassed, "I didn't mean to intrude deep into your thoughts. I apologize."

"You didn't, Ma'am," I reflected, "no apology needed. You caught me off guard and uncharacteristically silent. How rude of me. I'm usually a chatterbox." Elena seemed to want to retreat to the well-lit kitchen. I followed her and smiled at her uneasiness.

Leaning against the refrigerator, I finally admitted that I was well aware of the apartment and the building. I was not being snide.

"Ma'am, I grew up in this place. This was my home." The Realtor's mouth opened slowly and her eyebrows rose in awe. She took a deep breath.

"You grew up here?"

"Yes Elena . . . if I may call you by your first name, *I grew up here.*"

"Well . . . yes . . . please call me Elena. Holy cow! This must be like Christmas for you," she added. "You must be thrilled to revisit your homestead again. I mean, ya know . . . to actually reminisce and *to witness* the same views you saw as a child and especially in anticipation of the forthcoming Christmas season and holidays. Is it the same today, as it was when you lived here or you were a boy?"

"Yes, in many ways nothing has changed . . . *nothing.* I grew up here. In other ways, it's not the same at all—there are minor changes here and there. I suspect many people have lived here since I was a child. It was just my dad and me anyway. My mother died giving birth to me, but she conceived me in that room over there, I suspect," he voiced, while pointing a finger at the bedroom.

Elena spoke softly and whispered, "Mea culpa. I am so sorry for your loss; especially at a time when you needed your mother most, as a baby."

She hesitated.

"What was your mother's name?"

"Mary . . . Maria, to some," I responded, "just like the Madonna."

"She couldn't have had a better name," Elena reacted, smiling broadly. "Why don't I leave you here alone for a few minutes? I have a coffee in my car and can leave you to your thoughts."

"It's not necessary for you to go. I have seen what I needed to see, and perhaps we can go to Caffe Vittoria and grab a cappuccino."

"That'd be fine . . . let me get my bag and lock up. We can discuss the condo and the listing sheet over a cappuccino or cannoli, or tiramisu . . . my treat!"

"You're on," I replied. "I walked by the Caffe earlier and no one was around due to the weather. That is, except for two elderly men who were animated and arguing over a cup of cold coffee, I suspect. There were lots of hand gestures. Let's go see if they've killed each other yet," I suggested, in a vain attempt at humor.

"Yah . . . they may be dead by now," she laughed. "The old guys love to argue . . . keeps their blood pumping. It's Italian 'one-upmanship.'"

Chapter 3

My childhood friends, Aldo and Dominick, were around most days, especially during summer vacation. Don't get me wrong; we had *many* friends in the close neighborhood. Our home environment was not dissimilar to that of the old radio and TV commercials by the Prince Spaghetti Company in 1969. They operated a pasta factory in my neighborhood. I identified with the era because I lived on Prince Street as well. The commercial touted Prince spaghetti as the pasta of choice on Wednesdays—'Wednesday was Prince Spaghetti Day' and a mother was calling her son home for dinner. She was yelling, 'Anthony . . . Anthony,' which really sounded like *Antony!* He was shown running down the alley or street between the tenements and homes just to get home for a spaghetti dinner. A local kid who I seem to remember vaguely, Anthony Martignetti, starred in the TV version of the commercial. The vision of Anthony running still sticks in my mind to this day . . . I could envision see him hustling as fast as he could home to supper, all these years later.

Luigi Pastene and friends, of the famed Pastene Corporation, also started a business in the North End in 1870—they sold grocery products from Italy and expanded operations from their Fulton Street inception to the Northeast U.S., to Canada, Cuba and Naples, Italy in the early 1900s. Two successfully run companies began near my home as a child.

The coffee with Elena was finished early and she had another appointment or showing. She was covering for a colleague who had listed a commercial space on nearby Lewis Wharf. Commercial real estate was not her forté but a commission could be shared if she sold a listing on the commercial side.

*   *   *

I found Elena intriguing and attractive since she reminded me of Anna Maria Alberghetti, an Italian-born opera singer, TV and film star from my youth. Still alive, Alberghetti is in her early seventies. Elena's face was as pretty as Anna's and the hairstyle was similar. Elena indicated that she was a single mom of her daughter, Victoria who was in her twenties and away at Skidmore. She didn't elaborate on any more information about her personal life. She wore no wedding ring—I merely concluded that she was divorced.

I, being happily married for the second time, was not one to enable or encourage any personal conversation with *any* single woman. I had been there before. Living in Washington, Massachusetts and in the woods some 140-miles west of Boston, was my peace of mind. My wife, Susan was all I needed anyway—a woman sympathetic to a struggling writer of fiction and mystery. She had said that I would be the next Grisham, Patterson or Brown. Susan had the 'edit eye' for errors in context, grammar and spelling. She was an English major before I met her and taught for a while. She had no personal desire to write for herself but enjoyed comparing me to other writers of the day. As weird as John Irving wrote at times, Susan loved his work and thought my style of writing was similar to his.

Elena agreed that we should meet again to discuss any questions I might have on the listed property on Prince Street. She knew I was strongly interested in purchasing the piece in the North End and this opportunity was unique in that it was my childhood home. She found that to be the 'tipping point.' If I was to own a second property with access to Boston in general, it made sense that I would be attracted to my former residence, both for nostalgia sake and because it was known to me. My wife felt that it was serendipitous and yet fortuitous that I would see the listing at 76 Prince, and pursue the feasibility of us having a second abode in a familiar and fun place. The North End and Boston's downtown met that desire and appeal.

Elena gave the listing sheet to me. I knew the price would be expensive once the word, *condo* was added, to what was a basic apartment of old. That was the trend on the waterfront and on the streets of Little Italy. Two simple words (North End) meant high pricing. At an initial listing of $649,900, I was shocked until I saw the other local, harbor listings of two to four million dollars. *What a bargain,* I thought, to have your childhood home back in one's possession for ten to fifteen times more than your father had paid for it. Obviously a sign of the times, inflation and a ridiculous housing market now prevailed.

Elena could see the twinkle in my eyes after I mentioned that one of my prior novels showed promise on celluloid and the Hollywood industry of motion pictures. The novel was a historical fiction piece based on the Battle of Bunker Hill. A soldier and his lover were cast as the main characters and his death at Bunker Hill sparked a romance with the soldier's closest friend and the dead soldier's girlfriend.

The movie industry was apparently on a kick concerning any Revolutionary War and Civil War stories. Kevin Costner and others were leaning toward those kinds of tales and scripts. I had paid some $10,000 for a local screenwriter to convert my book into something that might appeal to film producers. The monetary advance from a major film company in L.A. meant that I was finally being noticed and that I had other novels worth looking at as well. The financial promise of a high percentage of the take at the box office meant I could seek out a second urban home for weekend jaunts if I desired. My wife and my eight-year-old son, Graziano, who was named after a distant cousin in Canada, encouraged me to rent a vacation home near a major city during the summer. It never happened.

The name, Graziano was a moniker that I had always wanted to have in the family—the beauty and mellifluous sound of it was compelling to me. Nothing was more beautiful and gracious than *that* Italian name. My son, a dark skinned boy in summer, was the epitome of my heritage although Susan was a mixture of French, Dutch, Italian and English. 'Grazie,' as we called him, inherited my olive-colored skin genes I guess.

It was early December and just after Thanksgiving, so I was in a hurry to close on this deal on Prince if it was meant to be. I knew from Elena that the owners only used the condo part time and resided in winter in Venice, Florida. They were anxious to move the property, according the Realtor. A rational and fair offer on the property would probably be considered strongly by the current owner. The listing had been on the market for almost a year. Price may have been the reason, or the fact that it stood near the end of the street adjacent to busy Commercial Street. The Charlestown Bridge was moments away near Polcari's Restaurant.

I walked Elena to her car, which was parked off Prince. She hugged me before departing and wished me a happy holiday season even if the deal did not go through as we had hoped. I still needed to determine an offer if I was serious and she would probably hound me daily for a bid on the property. She would get 7%.

"Buon Natale. Arrivideci. Ciao," she offered sweetly as she closed the door of the Nissan Maxima. I watched as she backed from the alley and drove away to the evening appointment awaiting her by the wharf. I had her business card and number and she had mine. I waved to the taillights of red, and turned toward Hanover Street.

*   *   *

I had always regretted committing a *mortal* sin, ever since I was a child of eight or so. Aldo and Dominick had dared me to steal something from Stracuzzi's Market near Fleet Street. It was a small shop and convenience store by today's standards. Mr. Stracuzzi was old and bald-headed, short and stocky, but very pleasant. He reeked of garlic and the store occasionally smelled of smoked or salted fish and dried calamari or scungili. A candy counter was three-tiered at the front of the store and had Italian treats, imported chocolates and domestic candy bars and gum. An open box of Double Bubble gum as single pieces was always available so kids could count out and purchase five or ten for one cent each.

After much teasing by my young peers, I entered the doorway of the store while Mr. Stracuzzi was in the back entertaining a customer with their order of breads and fish. Alone in the front and near the main door, I quickly copped a single piece of Double Bubble and stuck the small square in my coat pocket. Each one had a paper comic inside. *Guilt* set in as soon as I met my friends around the corner of the brick wall.

I had stolen!

I was a *Catholic* and now I was going to *Hell!* The idea that I had abused one of the Ten Commandments and disobeyed the word of God made me sick to my stomach. I couldn't return the piece. Mr. Stracuzzi would surely have been mortified and called my father. A priest would have been summoned to my home I thought, and then I would be dragged by the feet into a confessional in the nearby church. Penance would surely be many more *Hail Mary's* and more *Our Father's.*

Conveniently located was the St. Leonard of Port Maurice Catholic Church at Prince and Hanover. Too convenient, I thought. At the encouragement of and *pat on the bac*k from my friends, I opened the gum wrapper and devoured the tasty morsel in rapid fashion. It was stone hard and then slowly softened. The boys took the comic.

"How is it?" they asked, almost close enough to smell my breath.

"Good," I mumbled, my mouth feeling like I was chewing on putty. "It's good," I said, drooling.

After three or four minutes of chewing on the hard pink square, my teeth ached and I savored the sweet juice, only to spit the wad of evidence

into a nearby waste can at the corner of Clark and Hanover. The gum
wrapper I buried in the waste can as well.

The evidence was gone, the accolades by my friends were rowdy, and
my stomach ached from my obvious, *mortal* sin and guilt. *What had I done?
What the heck was I thinking?*

All these years later, I distinctly remembered the episode and never
confessed it to a priest on a Friday night at any church. This snowy night I
turned toward the front of the church property and studied the ornate doorway
and historic architecture. The sidewalk had not been cleared but I could hear
a church member or custodian shoveling the side stairs and steps. A note on
the door read that confessions were from 7 to 8 in the evening. Few footsteps
led to the heavy oak doors of old. The snow was deep. I took a chance and
turned the handle on the door to enter the front foyer. Stained glass windows
were everywhere. I remembered the basic interior from my youth, where my
father had me attend Sunday Mass and abstain from meat on Fridays. With
the loss of my mother, I was destined to attend weekly services religiously to
pray for the repose of her soul, and for mine as well.

The confessionals were to the sides of the back door, and a baptismal
marble basin held the holy water of a recent ceremony. It was the same
basin over which I was baptized.

The confessionals were ornate wooded booths with doors that separated
the confessor from the parishioners in the last two pews. One or two woman
with black veils knelt in prayer. I decided to sit next to one who's aged and
wrinkled hands were folded and intertwined with rosary beads. She fondled
one bead at a time, silently moving her lips in prayer. She repeatedly said the
Hail Mary and then the occasional *Our Father*. I felt the same apprehension
that I felt in my youth when I would tell the priest that I had sworn ten times,
disobeyed my father five times and had *impure* thoughts. The penance was
usually the same: 'My Son, say three *Hail Mary's* and five *Our Father's* with a
good *Act of Contrition*.' You could vary the list of sins but Father Santini always
had the same penance for kids it seemed. It must have been cathartic for him
to hear the sins of a child over those of the adults that had used the Lord's
name in vane or had committed adultery or grand theft. Christ loved children
and so did the priests in our parish. Both Father Santini and Father Ferrara
were the best ones to confess to. They never yelled like the others.

When my time came, I had butterflies abound. I entered the doorway
on the left and knelt before the screen that separated me from the priest. I
had no idea who he was. But in the dim light, I could see that he appeared
more like a Franciscan monk or Jesuit, smock and all.

"Bless me Father for I have sinned," I began. "I have but one sin to
confess after decades of my life. I believe it is a venial sin."

"Go on, my Son," he offered, sympathetically. He sat back and tilted his ear to the screen between us.

"Father, I grew up in this neighborhood and I'm an older man now, who has family of my own. I have not been back here in decades. It is by chance that I am here this week on business."

"Welcome home, my Son," he responded. "What sin is it for which you wish to be forgiven?" He seemed to care that I had returned to the neighborhood.

"When I was young Father, perhaps eight-years-old or so, I stole a piece of bubble gum from the convenience store across the street." He seemed to chuckle lightly but listened intently.

"The store was owned by a Mr. Stracuzzi and I was chided into stealing the gum by my two friends of the same age. The store remains today and has been renamed but I still have butterflies if I pass the doorway—even on this snowy night." I hesitated and he spoke.

"All these years my Son, you have carried that burden?"

"Yes, Father. I never confessed the sin and yet I received Holy Communion many times after the event. I basically received Christ but was not in the '*State of Grace.*'"

The priest sat back further and went momentarily silent. He then leaned against the screen of the confessional and whispered, "Son, do you think that Jesus was perfect—a perfect child? We know that he probably wasn't and that his mother and father had to discipline him on occasion. Not honoring thy father and mother was a sin."

"Yes, Father."

"I'm sorry that you have been burdened all these years for a sin that you think was venial and not *mortal*. We know that the Ten Commandments suggest that 'stealing' is a *mortal* sin, right?"

"Yes, Father it is a *mortal* sin."

"Son, I think that your penance has been partially met through your sincere guilt all these years. I consider your sin a venial one as well. I forgive you for this transgression 'in the name of the Father, the Son and the Holy Spirit.'"

"Thank you, Father for your understanding and absolution."

"I am happy for you and your period of Grace, my Son. Please say three *Hail Mary's* and five *Our Father's* and a good *Act of Contrition.*"

Holy crap! It was the same penance as in my youth! I smiled at the coincidence and began to leave . . . when he spoke softly through the screen, "Son? Was the gum tasty?"

"Yes it was, Father."

"Was it worth it? I mean . . . the taste?"

"No Father, it wasn't."

"Then go in peace, my Son and teach your children well. Guilt always follows . . . no matter what the crime is. God bless you."

"Grazie, Father," I responded, respectfully.

*   *   *

St. Leonard's was the first official church of all Italians and the first Roman Catholic Church in New England built by Italian immigrants as well, in 1873. The first pastor was Father Conterno and later, Father Guerrini of the Franciscans, finished the plans that the pastor had envisioned. The huge church had a Peace Garden on the grounds, a place to relax and to avoid the commotion of the daily activities in the North End. Inside, the grand stone arches were ornate and Italian in architectural styling—almost Roman. A half rotunda, coliseum-like, enveloped the altar like a half moon. Historically, the first marriage in the stone edifice was on September 12, 1873. Louisa Rappeto married Pietro Guidi.

St. Leonard's was not the oldest Catholic Church however. St Mary's of the Sacred Heart was built in 1834.

By the time I said my penance and left the church, more parishioners had arrived at the door and greeted me with, "Buono Sera." I replied, "Good Evening" as well and the smile on my face must have been the broadest of them all. In Catholicism, being cleansed from sins is the greatest feeling in the world and that was the feeling that I had at that very moment.

The man shoveling snow, leaning on a shovel, had stopped to say hello and I nodded to him, still smiling. He seemed perplexed by my demeanor but knew that I was in the *State of Grace*. The old Italians are devout and I didn't need to clarify why I was so happy. He knew why.

That night, I decided conclusively that I needed to purchase the home around the corner and introduce my wife and son to the church that I once held as mine. From baptism to First Communion, to Confirmation in my teens, *that* was the church that was my own personal history in life.

I would need to come back with my family even if it was only on special weekends or during school vacations. The house on 76 Prince Street would be the ticket to my memories of the past and there was ample room in the old abode to allow me to continue writing from a new perspective and renewed 'urban landscape' of potential prose. The sights surrounded me and could be inspirational to a wordsmith.

Chapter 4

During much of the writer's conference, my mind wandered back and forth to the North End. I wanted to proceed with the acquisition of my childhood home and make an offer. I reminisced about my youth and my close friends from school. We were tight for many years and lived each day by playing in local parks and hanging out at each other's home. A playground was located on Parmenter and North Bennett Streets and behind St. Leonard's Church. It was the first playground in the United States and appropriately in 1885, was only a pile of sand. It was designed to give children exercise. A modern playground evolved over the next century or so, with swings and seesaws.

One small park was located near the Paul Revere House. Revere was born in the North End. The park was near North and Fleet Streets as I recall. There was a wall to hit tennis balls off of and a basketball hoop or two. Graffiti sometimes graced the single wall of cement. I'm sure that Paul Revere would have been irritated at our abuse of his front yard and the now North Square (Plaza), a pleasant retreat of cobblestone walks and gardens in summer. The historical home of 1667 was a colonial gray clapboard building—one of the most impressive homes in all of Boston, small and reminiscent of the 1600-1700s. It is still lauded as downtown Boston's oldest building and one of the only remaining structures from the Colonial period in American history. Between that 'revered' patriot's home and the famed Old North Church (1723) between Salem and Unity Streets, much of Boston's history was set in the North End community. North Church remains the oldest church in Boston. As children, Dom, Aldo and I were immune to its relevance in the emergence of the New

World. We had to be reminded of the history in grade school and Jr. High. On April 18, 1775, a sexton in the church hung two lanterns from the steeple, a signal to Paul Revere to tell the locals that the British were coming by sea. Yet we children always felt a part of the Italian-American culture, but not necessarily the colonial history per se. How naive we were of the importance of the historic sites that encircled us.

Philadelphia, Plymouth Rock and Williamsburg, VA were to us the history of the United States and yet we avoided recognizing our own backyard for the birthplace of our nation. In winter, the coating of snow on the 'Paul Revere and horse' statue was a reminder of the patriot's impact on Boston. It is referred to as the Paul Revere Mall. We often tried to climb the icon. Nearby residents frequently shooed us away in disgust. We were kids and the North End in winter was a playground at every juncture of a street corner and park.

Each year near Fleet Street and North Atlantic Avenue, an Italian man would set up his Christmas stand of trees for sale. He was the same old gentleman that would sell spring and summer flowers under a red, white and green canopy/umbrella near Christopher Columbus Park. Sometimes he sold cold fruit by the piece for a quarter. Oranges, apples and bananas were usually laid out on a bed of crushed ice and sold next to buckets of seasonal flowers: daisies, carnations, lilies and roses.

The Christmas trees were said to be fresh cut locally and almost everyone in the North End checked out his prices on the balsams, pines, and other more treasured species, i.e. blue spruce. Spruce trees were at a premium, and costly to boot. At night, Mr. Lagasse had strings of white lights strung across tall 2" x 4"s, which cordoned off the perimeter of the sawhorses. The trees leaned back for best viewing. They were anywhere from 5-10 feet in height. The lights illuminated the boxed-in area where clients and patrons would spend time selecting the right tree for their apartments. They often took the trees home on a child's sled. The nighttime lighting also prevented anyone from stealing trees from a darkened corner. That was sure to happen when he was not looking or if he was preoccupied with a serious customer. It was sad, but some people stole the greenery during the holiday season. Wreaths and Christmas balls of pine bows, or red bows of felt, were absconded behind his back. Kids were usually the culprits—not us, but children from other neighborhoods.

Mr. Lagasse would run after the ones that he could see and hit them with a broom that he used to clear snow off the pines on display. He knew most of the children in the neighborhood and Lagasse was keen to call their parents at the end of the day. As he ran after them, he verbalized some unusual Italian expressions that were profane. Non-Italian speaking customers laughed at the old man behind his back and really had no idea

what he was calling the children that were obvious hooligans and thieves.
The local Italians, especially the women, covered their ears when he went
on a tirade. It was both comical and sad at the same time.

We children often brought Mr. Lagasse a hot cup of coffee from a local
shop. He could not leave his stand and his wife only made one Thermos
full of coffee for him a day. It was cold near the harbor and he looked
frozen. Customers bought his trees out of sympathy. In return for our
generosity, the old man would bring cookies to the homes of all of our
parents around Christmas. He was a proud Italian from Sicily and took
little crap from anyone, adult or child. He claimed to be a relative of the
infamous, New York Gambino family, so children thought he was Mafioso
in heritage. He wasn't.

*   *   *

The North End was known for festivals, especially in summer and
fall. There was music, festivities and dancing, parades and processions of
religious icons, special church occasions and revered saint celebrations.
We children always looked forward to the Feast of St. Anthony in August
and St. Lucy's Feast in September. There were local festivities in December
as well, but St. Anthony's was the highlight of the year.

For almost 90 years, Anthony was celebrated as the Patron Saint of
Lost and Stolen Articles. Italians would pray devoutly for the return of lost
items. I prayed for my mother who was 'lost' during my childbirth. It was
my own personal moment that I shared with no one.

Chapter 5

That night in my hotel room I could not sleep. I had bought a Starbucks in the lobby and hardly finished the strong-flavored concoction before attempting to grab some shut-eye. The hotel room was nothing fancy: the advertisement on the dresser claimed that a new mattress was being tested in all rooms. It was similar to the Visco 3000 that was popular on TV. I wondered how the mattress was being tested. Was it for sound REM sleep or for sex? I chuckled to myself and left no feedback since I hated surveys. People always lied just to mess them up.

It was 3:33 A.M. in the morning and I knew that the caffeine had caused my insomnia. I had been inspired to write by the prior evening's events—the potential new condo and the recollection of my youth, or at least to *begin* a new novel. The title eluded me but it would surely be about Christmas in the North End. All the visual and cultural 'sensory material' and fodder was there for the prose, the exposé and some minor dialogue. I didn't remember enough Italian from my youth to write it in that language. Both my father and my Uncle Frank had tried to teach me more of the native language of their forefathers. I did speak it fluently as a child but over the decades of living elsewhere as an adult, much of the (idiomatic) phrases were lost. I could barely get by now with a word or phrase or two, in Italian.

I lay awake in my underwear and crossed my arms behind my head. The pillow was inviting. I stared at the ceiling where a fan graced the center of the room. In winter it was of no use other than to send the heated air back down toward the floor if it was run in reverse. It lay silent during my deepest thoughts. The room was seventy degrees and comfortable.

The morning came fast and I had pretty much had it with the writer's conference. Today was scheduled to be a workshop of sorts. The instructors would chose a subject and ask the attendees or registrants to write a few short passages in an hour or less. They would then have you read your creation out loud in front of twenty of your peers. The classmates were to subsequently criticize or modify your ideas. What did they know? The exercise was more destructive in criticism than constructive. I had paid $400 for this horse-ticky and felt vain enough to know that I wrote *better* than most of them in the class, at least in my own mind. My time would be better spent back in the North End.

By 10 A.M., I was sipping coffee and eating a fresh cheese Danish in a café on Salem Street. The magic was back and the sun was warming on this early December day. I finished the pastry and marveled at the number of people that were either late for work or blowing the day off like I was. I laughed to myself.

I had already spoken on the phone with my wife and son back home. She was aware that I was on a mission but I shared little with my son, Grazie. He disliked change at his young age and I didn't want to frighten him with the news of a potential new home, or second home for that matter.

A free chair was available at my table. My long black wool coat was typically Italian in style and I was casually dressed in a sport shirt and dress slacks. I had on leather hiking boots, which were appropriate and waterproof for the inclement weather I had anticipated for the week of the writer's conference. The local TV station had predicted more snow but that wasn't even close to accurate. It had always amazed me that the TV weathermen or women actually got paid for being 50% wrong, almost daily.

Many of the sidewalks in the North End had been shoveled or plowed by the next day. The streets were naturally narrow (with or without cars being parked from the previous night) because the historic North End paths and drives were basically laid out and unchanged from the Colonial days and mid-1700s. The North End had an Old World feel to it. Many streets were still cobblestone and fabricated from granite blocks.

My coffee had grown cold as I studied the patrons and residents that seemed to have a routine of a non-committal agenda or destiny that early in the morning. The frequently spoken, 'Buon Giorno' was met with my similar reply. I always smiled and they didn't. The natives knew I wasn't from Boston. They sensed my style of dress was from 'out of town' and there was a level of uncertainty, perhaps mistrust. I looked Italian but I was overly friendly, I suppose. I preferred to study the interior of the old shop, the brick walls and scenic art from Venice, Florence or Sorrento. There were numerous prints and *I* was the only one looking at them . . . hence I was not *from* there!

A stroll down Salem Street brought back many memories. I had grown up basically around the corner from my close friend, Aldo Spinelli. He lived on Salem Street as a child. I passed one or two restaurants and then came upon a storefront that startled me. It read in gold letters on a black background:

Spinelli's Tailoring and Shoe Repair
Aldo Spinelli, Jr.
Fine Italian Leather Repair

I was shocked at the sight of the sign. Aldo, I had recalled, was the first in his family with the name, 'Aldo.' This would perhaps be his son. Italian leather was 'to die for' but most shops that dealt with the commodity were on Newbury Street near the Theatre District, not in the North End. Many men and women 'of fashion' desired leather shoes and coats. The prices were exorbitant on Newbury Street and the sales people were stuffy and arrogant.

My heart raced in anticipation that Aldo Jr. might know where my classmate and best friend, Aldo Sr., was today. I entered only to hear the sound of an aging commercial sewing machine (a 1930s Singer) clicking away from low oil or little lubrication. The head of a forty-year-old man was bowed in his work. It was warm in the shop and leather straps, shoes, pocketbooks, and coats hung from hangers or were stacked on top of one another in piles. All seemed to need repair. The smell of shoe polish permeated the room. A small counter top, well-worn Formica, greeted the customer and slips of paper with notes on them were stuck in the shoes tied together in pairs. He was backed up with work.

"Buon Giorno," he said, hardly lifting his balding head. "Can I help you?" he continued. I was quick to respond in English. "Good Morning. I'm John Perri and was wondering if you were related to an old friend of mine—Aldo Spinelli from the 1950s. Might that be your father? I see you are a junior."

"Yes Sir. My father was Aldo, Sr."

My heart dropped. "Was?" I responded, with sadness.

"Yes, Sir." he replied in a lower tone. He pointed to a faded color photo on the wall near his desk. "He was killed in Vietnam in 1965." Junior must have thought me weird or emotional as a tear or two welled up in my eyes.

"Your father was my best friend as a child. I used to live on Prince, and we grew up together." Aldo, Jr. rose and came around the counter. He hugged me and was silent for a good ten seconds.

"I'm sorry for the bad news, Mr. Perri. He often spoke of you and he wondered where you went when you left the North End. I'm over his loss.

Pardon me please but I was a *youngster* when he died. I hardly knew him and there are few photos from the war. My mother wouldn't hang them on the wall or display them. She hated the war and the loss of her husband. She passed on a few years ago and was miserable to that day, without him. They were lovers and friends. Her name was Constance 'Connie' Spinelli. Her maiden name was Connie DiNardi. She grew up here and you may well have known her."

I hesitated and wiped my eyes with a tissue. "Yes, I knew them both. I'm sorry for your loss." Junior asked me to sit in a chair that was reserved for customers who had quick shoe repairs or needed unique rawhide laces for boots and heavy work shoes. They often would have soles or heels replaced in a short ten minutes time.

We chatted and reminisced about our lives, the lives of two kids in the poorer section of Little Italy. By the end of the conversation, both of us were laughing and became very close. I promised to visit his father's grave and to say a prayer for his parents. All of the while that we were engrossed in conversation I held the framed 8" X 10" photo in my hands. Aldo Jr. had taken it down from the shelf for me to observe up close. It was the typical soldier photo from 'Nam. He was a helicopter pilot and his foot rested on the step to the cockpit. He held a rifle across his body and a cigarette dangled precariously from his mouth. I reminded his son that we used to smoke behind the building we were in, even as teenagers. Cigarettes were twenty-five cents a pack for Camels, non-filtered. We laughed until we cried. No other customers came in and we exchanged addresses and phone numbers. He offered me coffee but I took a rain check. I told him I would be back soon and that my plans were to purchase a home in the North End again. He smiled.

"I live in my father's place," he spoke, with pride. "I see the Perri home on Prince is up for sale, or at least part of it."

"Yes, I hope to buy it," I smiled from ear to ear.

"Too much, Johnnie!" he said, raising an eyebrow. I hadn't been called 'Johnnie' for many decades. I felt at home with my best friend's son. It was cathartic and overpowering. I was as comfortable with him as I had been with his father. The physical looks were similar.

Aldo Jr. told me of the gravesite location in the Copp's Hill Burial Ground. It was moments away and the second oldest cemetery in Boston. I hugged him and said goodbye.

"I will be back before Christmas," I promised. He smiled, broadly. I was like a long lost relative to him, at least in his mind. And we *were*, I suppose. His father and I were blood brothers having pricked our fingers and touched them together as foolish teenagers during our crazy days at Eliot Middle School on Charter Street.

Chapter 6

The unexpected encounter with Aldo's son was overpowering for me and I wondered what had happened to Dominick Russo, as well. That would be for another time perhaps, since I forgot to ask Aldo, Jr. I was sure he would know and I would be returning within two to three weeks anyway.

I walked slowly down Salem, past Bennett, Sheafe and Hull Streets. I came upon a floral shop called Fratello's Flowers. I purchased two red roses and was hopeful that I could find the graves of Aldo and Connie.

Junior might not have known that his father and mother were lovers in school, childhood sweethearts. I remembered Connie well and Aldo confided in me when she became pregnant as a teen. They were young and scared. I don't know if Aldo, Jr. was the result of that conjugal encounter in the backseat of Aldo's father's car, or whether Connie *went away* for a while. I seem to remember that she was absent from school for months and the rumor was she was ill. Being *ill* back then or *visiting an aunt* were expressions that adults used when teenagers, who were *with child,* went away to have a baby—generally they were given up for adoption. As a Roman Catholic, premarital sex or 'going all the way' was a no-no—a *mortal* sin with a penance far greater and worthy of more than three *Hail Mary's* and five *Our Father's!*

Heavy "petting" was also confessed with absolution granted, and teenagers confessed those sins often. Teenage pregnancy was the ultimate transgression, short of murder! Sex outside of marriage was 'super *mortal.*' After all, hormones superseded common sense and the use of contraception was a sin, as well. Abortion was unheard of back then. Unless junior was created from a teenage pregnancy, he was probably conceived later on in their relationship, soon after their marriage. His current age favored the later birth.

*   *   *

Copp's Hill Burial Ground (formerly Windmill Hill) stood out, even in the heaviest of snowfalls. Many stones were above the recent white storm of white, fluffy powder. The cemetery history was one of three major notable places in the North End. Geographically, it was a portion of the 'original' Boston and the stones were from the Revolution and earlier. It dated back to 1659 and was named after William Copp, a shoemaker, who once owned the land.

Robert Newman, the sexton who placed the signal lanterns in the steeple of the Old North Church is immortalized there. Buried also are thousands of immigrants of Irish, Italian and even Jewish descent. Soldiers, British and American, may be found there, heroic deaths of the nearby Revolutionary battles.

The British used the hill as a lookout toward Charlestown and Bunker Hill during the Revolutionary War. It has the same view today of Charlestown and the U.S.S. Constitution (Old Ironsides, 1797), the oldest commissioned ship in the U.S. Navy still afloat and the 'ship of state.' It is berthed in Charlestown Naval Yard to this day, for sightseers to board. Paul Revere provided her copper bolts. An Armenian immigrant, Moses Gulesian offered money to save her. The 'people' followed suit with donations and she was saved from demolition. The ship, once destined for Navy target practice, is motored out each year and 'turned around' during the Fourth of July holiday week. It was, in a way, a maritime accomplishment of the North End and harbor peoples.

Surprisingly, Copp's Hill contains the remains of many residents of the North End and many African-Americans who lived in what was known as the *New Guinea Community*. Prince Hall, an anti-slavery activist, is interred there. Many blacks are buried in unmarked graves. I have often wondered if that same word, 'guinea,' referred to the slang/ slur for an Italian, *a guinea*.

History or folklore tells us that the origin of the slang word may have to do with the willingness of Italians to work for 'one British pound and a schilling'—a British guinea, a trivial amount. The word, guinea also referred to dark-skinned peoples, both Blacks and Italians. Interestingly enough, the word was no better than the epithet, 'wop' that erroneously was thought to mean 'without papers.' Many Italians had no papers to identify themselves when they arrived, however that was not the true origin of the word, *wop*.

It really referred to people who were members of a criminal organization in Italy. It is the English word for that organization, 'Guappo.'

The North End cemetery of note was much larger than it appeared from afar and resided between Charter, Hull and Snowhill Streets. On this one particular day, *Snowhill* was more than a street name. I was determined to find the grave of my friend. Aldo, Jr. was kind enough to write down the section and row of the Spinelli family memorial stone. Junior had indicated that it was quite large and there were extra plots as needed for other family. Aldo was not ready for that future but desired ultimately to be there when the time came.

He had mentioned that he always placed a wreath there in December, and a U.S. flag waved each day in honor of his father. His father was a veteran and Aldo was determined to have that national recognition of his service and death, outside Saigon.

Aldo's chopper was shot down and seven servicemen were killed. He escaped momentarily and was later captured, tortured and shot, by all accounts of the military. Some people claimed that he was killed by 'friendly fire' but that was never confirmed.

I was pained at the thought of his demise and the Vietnam War, in general. He was bright and surely had a future beyond his military service. Flying helicopters was no small feat. His dog tags were displayed at the shoe shop and I held them in my hands, briefly . . . weeping profusely. There was a reason why we called it an 'unnecessary war.' Aldo was a patriot and never expected to die, I'm sure. He was a modern day Paul Revere.

At the gate to the cemetery, I stood and perused the view of the dead and slate and granite markers of varied ages and conditions. Some stones were leaning and had lichen-encrusted growth, a parasite on certain memorials. It generally thrives on air like Spanish moss. Moisture, nutrients and minerals, basically dust in the air, provide the nutrition that eventually encroaches on porous stone and can conceal the names and dates of the deceased, disrespectfully.

The row I sought was # 13 and that, in and of itself, was ominous in its own right. The number is unlucky to most people. I was up to my shins in snow and didn't care. My pant legs and socks were wet and chilled, evidence that snow had entered my boots at the top of the laces. I tried to count the stones and knew that the SPINELLI marker was supposed to be number 17 in the ever rambling, uneven row. Aldo, Jr. had promised me that I would see the memorial easily from afar. An angel with rising hands toward heaven was atop the granite marker, he had added as a clue.

The angel, a flag and wreath was easily discernable from afar and I was drawn to the stone by persistence and by *fate*. It was distinctive and a true eternal testimony to Aldo Jr.'s mother and father.

Once again, I felt remorse, but consolation in finding my dead friend. I stood in silence as I listened to traffic on Commercial Street. The road wasn't far away and the occasional horn distracted me from my silent thoughts and prayers. I was not a devout man but always said a *Hail Mary* and an *Our Father* at gravesites—any one of note, through friendship or direct relation. I was alone and foolish in many ways to have trekked through the snow shortly after a blizzard the day before. By now, my feet were almost numb from the cold, akin to my remorse and thoughts of his unnecessary loss.

Foolishly freezing my toes, I cleared the base of the monument of snow and knelt on one knee. I placed both roses, each wrapped in pink paper and accompanied by baby's breath and ferns, on the stone base. They would wilt or even harden in hours since roses were as fragile as the human bodies buried below. They would surely blacken at the tips from the freezing cold—the green leaves would curl and become rigid. The next snowfall would ultimately hide them and I knew they would be gone in spring. The gesture was merely that . . . a gesture of love for my childhood friend and his wife.

I felt exhausted as I stood and touched the angel on top of the stone. It stood some ten inches high and appeared fragile. Her face was beautiful and I swore that I saw a tear in her eye. The face was cameo-like and the tear was actually melting snow from the sunlit top of her hair. For a moment, I had sensed the miracle that people often experienced in religion. The angel was crying. I was wrong and foolish. Melting snow was not tears, merely the previous night's accumulation transforming into water. There was no salt in these fake tears, fabricated in my mind. The only salt that was real was from the tears that I tasted on my lips as I wept. They had rolled down my cheeks and by my lips. Other pearls seemed frozen on my cheek.

"Welcome home," I said out loud, for no one else to hear. "Welcome home, blood brother."

I have always said, 'Welcome Home' to any Vietnam veteran that I've met in my life. They were treated terribly in word and in person when they returned, either alive or dead in the late 1960s and 70s. I have never failed to welcome them or show respect. Each one always said, 'Thank you.' It's the least we can do for the living veterans of the past. Fifty-five thousand of them died for us, and their names are on a 'wall' in Washington, DC.

I looked around after having read the accolades, dates and names on the Spinelli memorial. I memorized his service dates, his date of birth and death and kissed the angel's head. Turning around, I no longer heard any local traffic. I was immune to the extraneous confusion and sounds.

I would return in the spring when the hill was unencumbered. The next time I would have my family with me. That would be informative for Susan and Graziano who had never known the Spinelli's but knew they meant a lot to me when I was young. I bowed to the stone and said,

"Arrivideci amico, Aldo . . . and Connie. Riposare bene . . . rest well." I managed to retrace my steps in the snow. My feet were too numb to be pained. My heart hurt more than my feet at that moment.

Chapter 7

I drove west on the Massachusetts Turnpike, at the typical 70 MPH speed and basically zoned out on the ride. I was headed home to Washington at the opposite end of the 'Commonwealth.' It always intrigued me that Massachusetts was a commonwealth and not a *State*. Few others had that accolade. The conference in Boston had left me cold and it was more productive to visit the Italian North End than to sit through lectures. After all, I had a renewed interest in penning a new novel and my mind and focus was on the development of characters and the visions of a setting in Boston. The surroundings of the North End in winter gave me fodder for the exposé for which I needed—people, places and objects to expound upon. As I drove, I reflected on the past couple of days.

I had managed to say a few prayers at St. Leonard's before departing. I had promised Aldo's son that I would. I was in the front pew and virtually alone when I prayed briefly to the Patron Saint of that specific church. The statue of the Madonna was nearby and I recalled Mary from my youth, her holding the infant, Jesus. I am not a deeply religious person and in fact I am a non-practicing Roman Catholic—*once* a Catholic, *always* a Catholic I suppose, whether or not one attends church on Sundays as is customary. I'm back on the '*mortal* sin' list for having not attended Mass all these years. I was absolved of my 'bubble gum sin' and that appeased me. The episode would surely end up as an anecdote in my next fictional opine.

I was drained from the experience at the leather shop and the visit to the cemetery. My own parents weren't even buried there and yet I felt obligated to find Aldo, Sr., dead or alive. Peace of mind set in. My own parents were interned west of Boston in a small town where my mother had relatives.

She had died young during my birth from *post partum* hemorrhaging and I visit her cemetery in Sudbury on occasion. In modern day obstetrical procedures, and with *post partum* compression of the abdomen and hemostasis, the death of my mother probably would not have happened. It saddened me to have lost her as a mom and for my father to lose his loving wife and companion. My birth could not replace her and he lamented that he was lucky to have me but he had lost someone dear to him. He never remarried and my mother's photo was on his nightstand until his death. The road west reminded me of his pain and loss. Introspectively, I was becoming more nostalgic in my older age.

Why would I seek out my boyhood home? Why find Aldo? Why dwell on my childhood life and my mother? It was nostalgia . . . and it was my reality check, I suppose, for my own forthcoming mortality. We all sleep *alone* in the end.

*   *   *

My home in the town of Washington is located on Washington Mountain and just off Route 8. We are tucked back in the woods like folksinger, Arlo Guthrie whose father was the famed, Woody Guthrie. He lives there as well and raised his family there. Guthrie has a farm not far from us but we don't cross paths all that much—perhaps at the local gas station on occasion, or at the post office.

Washington is southeast of Pittsfield and near Beckett. The surrounding Berkshire Hills are mountain ranges that encompass Lee, Stockbridge, Lenox (home of Tanglewood), Adams and North Adams for starters. One has heard of Stockbridge in the lyrics from the James Taylor tune, *Sweet Baby James*. *Alice's Restaurant Massacree* was Arlo's unfortunate, personal experience in song—describing at length in humor and ridiculousness a confrontation with a local policeman, Officer Opie. It was about a case of 'littering' on some back road in Stockbridge, the town of beloved, and the late, resident artist, Norman Rockwell.

Exiting the Massachusetts Turnpike, one has only to ride local Route 8 North to find our abode. The town post office knows our address well should one get lost on Washington Mountain Road, Main Street or Lover's Lane. Our home is just off Stone House Road. The surrounding back roads converge like a spider's web; all intertwine centrally but they are limited in number and length.

I was inspired to move there *to write*. The scenery predisposes to good material for novels—peace and tranquility and my son, Grazie is able to grow up without much negative peer influence by kids of broken homes, troubled teens or a bastion of drug influenced, or alcoholic dominated families. My wife, Susan and I love the simplicity of the regional environment.

The town of Washington was founded in 1760 and was incorporated in 1777. Oddly, it mimics the timeframe of the important history of the North End. The revolutionists migrated west of Boston seeking places to farm and establish and nourish their own identity for independence and a quality life for their families.

Washington is only thirty-nine square miles in geography and the population has remained steady and stable at less than 600 people. The politics is 'open town meetings,' simple and uncluttered. It's 99.45% Caucasian; I suppose Ivory soap-like (i.e. 99 and 44/100% pure). It reeks *too pure* in a way to most folks, since only 0.37% and 0.18% are African-American and Hispanic, respectively. *How can a town have percentages of less than one percent of any ethnicity, or any nationality?* Washington, Massachusetts does. *What about the Italians? Are we less than 1% as well?* Perhaps, but we are not relevant to the census.

Like Susan and me, the town is mostly married couples (65% or so) with a median income of about $54,000. It offers little in the way of community services and Beckett seems to be the next town with offerings of necessities or staples to survive week to week. Nearby Pittsfield has a Wal*Mart and Lowe's and, of course, the mandatory Home Depot.

In winter, Washington offers a tree lighting ceremony during the holidays where people gather in the town center and sing carols and greet one another for the holidays. It's a family event and kids usually pepper each other with snowballs or sled on a nearby hill. The town tree is covered with lights that the fire department personnel and a ladder truck help adorn. The truck facilitates access to the top of the towering Colorado blue spruce. The shapely tree has been there for years, seventy-five or more and commemorates the name of a prior resident, who impacted the town in many ways. He was a well-liked town moderator, or noted selectman, for decades. The name was Beale. He lies in peace in a local cemetery in the nearby foothills, where there is a stone wall and iron gate defining and protecting the remains of many people from the 1700s and 1800s. He is in good company and each year at Christmas an anonymous person places a wreath at his grave. Someone leaves an empty brandy glass as well—we're not sure why. Beale's ghost has a secret annual tradition like 'Poe,' apparently. It's all part of the holiday week in town.

There's also a winter parade that lasts about five minutes but the young children love it. Hay wagons are provided by the local farmers and decorated by residents for fun, some rigs also classically pulled by horses. Loaded with hay, the kids can ride and sing to their hearts' delight. Someone, usually Mr. Fowler, plays Santa and rides in a stationary sleigh on a local, flatbed truck that Mr. Mitchell drives each year. He runs and operates an automobile repair service and gas station during the day. The parade is not a religious one but some people manage to attend holiday services or a parish potluck supper in conjunction with the weekend festivities at the local Protestant church.

*   *   *.

The Italian North End of my youth had many festivals and parades during the year. They were not always associated with the Christmas holidays but took place in August or September. They still remain today. Aside from the historic St. Anthony's or St. Lucy's Feasts, the North End celebrates a Fisherman's Feast of the Madonna Del Soccorso di Sciacca in August and the easier to say, North End pre-Christmas, Trellis Lighting ceremony in November. It's held in nearby Christopher Columbus Park and located adjacent to Boston Harbor and the present day Marriott. The trellises, a central portion of the park, tastefully enclose a monument and the walkways overlooking the harbor.

The North End encompasses many wharves with homes, condos and businesses that jut out into the harbor jetties. Festival lights are prominent and offer continuity for Battery and New Atlantic Avenues and Cross Street. The camaraderie at Christmas seems to make *everyone* 'Italian' for the moment and ethnically combines the Irish, Italian and Portuguese cultures and histories that were responsible for the founding of the original Boston neighborhoods. That included the numerous fishing ports, unique dialects, and closely knit neighborhoods of the first immigrants as well as the original American Revolution of the 1770s.

Part of my reasoning for acquiring the old homestead in Little Italy was to have my own child have the experience that I had remembered. Washington could not accommodate, in their infrequent celebrations, the ethnicity and festival-like atmosphere that Grazie might absorb intellectually in Boston. Although he was born in the Berkshires, I wanted him to know of the 'roots' of his Italian grandparents in the North End.

At 5 P.M., I finally arrived at our home. It seemed like no time at all to get there, a perception achieved in part by my recollections and thoughts of the last few incredible days. The first one to greet me at the car was now my son. It used to be Rusty, the Golden Retriever who was much faster than Grazie. Since the dog's passing a year earlier, Grazie was the only one to hurry to the driveway while Susan stood in the doorway. It was good to be home. Although I was a Boston native, my home was now in the Berkshire Mountains.

*　*　*

The following day, I contacted Elena and made a non-committal verbal offer on the property on Prince Street. I had plans to have Christmas there this year, if doable. A personal mission was in the cards and the excitement was mounting. Even if I had to rent the place before the paperwork needed for the closing was complete, I envisioned us being there for the holidays and would make every effort to accomplish that feat.

Chapter 8

My friend, Dominick Russo was a bit heavy in grade school. He often ate too much pasta and his mother was one to make sure that he never went hungry. The whole family including his dad and younger brother, Joseph didn't hold back on second helpings of dinners and desserts. I never personally teased Dom about his weight but many kids in school were unkind—often calling him 'fatso,' or 'a tub of lard.' Our days playing on the local basketball court did not help him in weight reduction. He would sit on the sidelines and rest from time to time, totally winded. I sympathized with him (at each time out) and encouraged him by saying that I felt winded too. I don't think he ever believed me. I was not breathing hard or heavily and I was in good physical shape back then.

Dom's mom, Angelica, always offered to make lunch for us. She was devout in her religion and went to Mass every day. At 7 A.M., she was there with her friends sitting in the front pew. I never heard her swear or make fun of anyone. His father, Julius named his son, Dominick Julius Russo after the singer, Julius LaRosa, and Julius often drank too much wine. He slept a lot, even during the day. Chianti was his undoing and he passed away from liver disease (cirrhosis) when we were young. Angelica prayed for Dom's dad every day.

It was Dom's father who took my dad and me for a tree each year. He would often say it was 'Albero de Natale Day,' meaning that it was time to get the Christmas tree. My father would come along, making it four, and we'd drag two sleds to the nearby parking lot to pick out and buy a freshly cut tree.

Since my birthday was close to Christmas and in early December, we made it a point of seeking out a nice balsam or spruce on the 'actual' day of my birth. We would have a party later in the day. Dom's father committed the date to memory. Back then, a tree was four or five dollars for a seven-footer, maybe less. Today's trees can run thirty-five to fifty dollars unless you cut your own at a local tree farm. There's one farm near Beckett, but we, as a family, always went into the woods by our home to find our own—fresh, full and tall. To this day, we use the same sled that I used with my father to transport it, a Flexible Flyer. The sled rails always had a yearly collection of rust but the red-brown corrosion disappeared after a while, especially when dragged over the hard, abrasive snow and ice. Steel wool worked just as well.

Grazie uses it to slide down a hill in the backyard all winter and then it's relegated once again to the hooks on the garage wall for another year of oxidation back to rust.

Dom, Aldo and I were always together during the holidays. We shopped at nearby stores before they became a mall of sorts at Faneuil Hall. We bought each other ornaments every Christmas. Many were ornate Italian glass balls that we hung on smaller trees, ones we had in our own bedrooms. Multicolored strings of lights were placed on each tree. We tried to outdo each other, a kind of rivalry. Each year we added more light sets.

We were like 'The Three Musketeers,' bonded by youth, but close schoolmates and friends to the end. Fistfights were few and arguments infrequent.

I still put their gifts on my family Christmas tree; the name we knew in Italian as, *Albero de Natale*. Why I am waxing nostalgic all these years later, I don't know. My life in the North End was so innocent for the most part that I hated to lose the tradition of anything that we did as kids. I have tried to pass those traits on to my son. Susan and I are catalysts for him, inspiration for his future. May he start his own memories so that when he grows up, and has a family of his own, he will seek out a Christmas tree using the same worn out sled of our past; an heirloom of significance.

Dominick was a sentimental person. He would often ask, 'Do you think we will always live here in Little Italy? I do.' He called it 'LI' for short and we all thought we'd stay there forever. We were young and naive but dedicated friends.

"Sure," I would respond. "Why would we move? All the sports teams are nearby." He was right to ask because we all loved the Red Sox and Celtics back then. Dom, due to his size, had large arms—could hit the ball a country mile. Everyone who teased him because of his weight, never wanted him to be on the *other side's* team, only their own.

More than once, Dominick accidentally broke a front window in someone's home with a hard hit, long ball. His massive biceps and quick timing did it. We never tried to retrieve the ball, in sharp 'cinema-like' contrast to the kids who jumped the junkyard fence in the movie, *The Sandlot*. In that movie, the challenge was to get back the infamous prized Babe Ruth-autographed ball before a junkyard-protecting dog named, *The Beast*, got to the ball before *them*. It's a must see movie for all baseball fans, young and old.

Dominick never cared to retrieve any ball.

'Shit,' he'd say in Italian (merda) and *run like heck*, hoping the neighbor would never figure out who had done the evil deed. He shook himself scared in his bedroom all night in anticipation of hearing his parents scream,

"Dominick! Did you break a window today? The neighbor says you did! They just called."

"No Mama," he'd lie, "Johnnie did it." The trouble was, there was no Johnnie that did it. Johnnie was *me*. At any rate, his mother would defend him to the end because Dominick was her little boy and she believed him. He never lied, at least in her mind. That's when the phone would ring at my house and *I* got the *interrogation*. I would cover for Dom and my dad would pay for the replacement window. He knew I didn't do it but he knew even more that Dom would be in serious trouble. Dom's dad would never be easy on Dom's 'behind.'

I was Dominick's closest friend and we often protected one another. That same kind of bonding seems to be lacking today in children. The blame tends to be on the other person, even to the point of lying.

*   *   *

We loved Christmas and many children our age had not yet come to grips with the legacy of Santa Claus. At eight-years-old, or even nine, some of us wanted to believe that Santa was the real deal. No one wanted to doubt that fact in fear of not receiving any presents each year. We were all Catholic and knew the true meaning of Christmas—the birth of baby, Jesus. On the other hand, we knew that gifts were brought to all children, especially the younger ones that had no concept of what Bethlehem and the Virgin Mary were all about.

Reinforcing that philosophy, Santa was all too real to us and we anxiously wanted to see him or tell him our Christmas wishes in the public arena. The local, historic Faneuil Hall was the site that we walked to, to meet Mr. Claus and sit on his knee. The Quincy Market rotunda was decorated like the North Pole and we truly believed he was the person who would come back on Christmas Eve and shower us with all the presents that we asked for. The list we gave to him, handwritten, was always returned to our parents in a covert manner. In this case, it was my father who eventually knew my secret wishes. He was in on the secret pact and that helped 'Santa' come close to meeting the items on the list. They were in cahoots!

In the North End, and in our Italian custom, our stockings were hung the night before Christmas. Not all of us had a fireplace, which posed a huge problem for the 'Big Man.' I hung my stocking on a shelf in the living room or placed it in a chair. We had no fireplace mantle, not even a fake one to simulate a chimney and hearth.

If you were good all year, you might receive fruit, an orange or apple and maybe some candy in the sock. My mother had knitted the stocking for me before I was born. She apparently loved Christmas and embroidered my name on the white border top of the red sock. If a child was bad, he or she often received two or three lumps of coal in the sock. That was not desired of course, but the supply of black chunks was easily acquired in the cellar—a coal bin was there. Any coal in the stocking made a devastating point!

Many homes were heated with coal. I pretty much got the fruit and candy or the occasional marzipan cookie. The cookies looked like fruit and were almond-flavored. Once in my life, I received a little of both, having been mischievous a month prior to the holidays. My father was proud of me in school and as a young person. He didn't need to reprimand me very often. He had it tough enough just trying to put food on the table as well as being both 'a mother and father' to me during the critical, formative years.

One tradition that stood out memorably in our home, and in those homes of my friends (who didn't have fireplaces for Santa to enter their homes), was a novel substitute for Santa's easy access.

"How will Santa get presents to me?" I would ask, in rational thought. "There's no chimney at 76 Prince Street." I was wrong. There was one but it was for the coal furnace not the home living space.

"He will come in through the door," Papa would say, reassuringly. He always had the answer and would smile. "Don't worry."

"But Father, we *lock* the hallway door." Again, he would reiterate,

"Not to worry, Santa has ways to get to our tree."

"How?" I asked, with my dubious, natural mind.

"Son, we have a 'Santa Key,' a 'Christmas Key' of sorts and then he would say it in Italian—*La Chiave di Natale.*

I loved the sound of that phrase—*La Chiave di Natale.* My father would open a secret door in the closet and pull out a brass key all shiny and polished. It had a red ribbon tied through the end where there were two holes. It reminded me of an old-fashioned railroad key or clock key, or even the key to a lock on a trunk. I knew then that Santa could still come in through the front door. Santa was magical, he reminded me.

There was a hook outside the front door jam. My father would ask me to hang the key on the hook. We would never have left our front door *unlocked* at night, Lord forbid. We didn't live in a bad neighborhood but we always locked the door for safekeeping. On the center of the door we always had a natural pine wreath or a grapevine-shaped heart complete with golden Christmas balls or a red bow. *The Christmas Chiave* was hung to the side of the door in plane view. Santa never missed it.

I was pretty smart but not savvy enough to realize that the key was too big for our lock, or that a robber could *also* use it to enter the foyer and kitchen. I trusted my father to the bitter end and knew that Santa was the only one to use the *special* key.

Dad's explanation was good enough for me, and other friends believed the yearly scenario as well. One friend, Ricardo, who lived three blocks away, had a real fireplace in his apartment. He expected Santa to arrive in that fashion until, one day he looked up the chimney and realized how *small* the flue was. The damper made it even smaller. When he questioned his parents, they told him that Santa was magical and could shrink to fit, complete with his bag of toys. Ricardo believed it and we followed and believed the story as well. No one dared to question how the jolly man got in. Doubting Santa was a no-no.

*   *   *

I have often wondered what happened to my own 'key'—*La Chiave di Natale*. I never came across it while sorting through my mother and father's belongings after he passed away. Having lost my mother at birth, she was not around to witness our annual tradition. It may have been buried in the boxes of ornaments and lights that were in his attic, yet I thought I had searched through everything and assumed that it was lost. I longed for the shiny brass artifact that held and captured my imagination for so many of my early years. About all that was left was a memory and a vision of the doorway where it once hung.

Chapter 9

Susan was happy to have me home from Boston. My return from the writer's conference was welcomed and she was affectionate, having missed me. The feeling was the same for me.

Early winter is tough and she was inundated with trying to entertain our son, Graziano and keeping up with the day-to-day household duties, laundry, shopping and Grazie's school needs. The driveway, which was extensive in length, had yet to be plowed from the recent storm that had occurred while I was traveling. She had learned to call Norman from the local gas station, especially when I was away. Sometimes he was busy. I normally plowed our drive with my old Chevy, a vehicle that had seen better days, even years.

We chatted in bed after our son had gone to sleep. She wanted to know more about the house that I had grown up in and how we would manage two homes if we purchased the second one. Our relationship was very close and she was amorous as well. We managed to get reacquainted that night and she was the same lover that I had always known. She enabled my senses, mentally and physically and the remote Washington home was comfortable for both of us.

My writing increased after we had moved there. Our closeness was always a priority. Honesty was paramount and our son had been conceived in a series of loving moments, some inside the home and some outside on a blanket under the stars.

Susan had already decorated the interior of the house for Christmas, except for a tree. It was early December but she liked the festive atmosphere of the old Cape we had purchased years earlier. We resided on forty acres and that alone was impressive. It was mostly woods but the back ten acres were still grass—grass that I mowed with an old John Deere. The tandem mowers kept the property neat and attractive. A white, wooden fence surrounded the property, a yearlong project for a solitary guy at the helm. Susan helped me assemble the longitudinal rails after the postholes had been dug and posts cemented in place. Fortunately, the left side of the property bordered another man's land and no fence was required. He had created a three-foot stone wall from the clearing of the land to farm and raise corn. He had a few head of cattle and sustained the herd on his summer corn and tall grass. His acreage was over a hundred and he was a pleasant neighbor, thoughtful and sharing at harvest time. His vegetables were the best.

The backyard slope was gradual but long and we allowed Grazie and his friends to slide on our own property. There were few boulders or oaks as obstructions and he avoided them masterfully when sliding with his friends. I had rigged up an old truck 'carcass' and rear end pulley fabricated from the back left wheel. We fashioned a rope tow from marine quality braid, a twisted heavy roping to get them up the hill on their skis. The truck sat at the top of the incline and a pulley attached to a short telephone pole looped the thick rope around the top and bottom rigging. First gear was just the right speed for pulling the kids to the top. They grabbed the rope gently, then firmly and hung on for dear life. In a minute or two, they were at the summit.

Susan could watch them easily out the bay window in the kitchen. Grazie knew how to start the truck and engage the clutch and the stick shift into first gear. The worst part of the experience was traipsing up the hill with a five-gallon can of gas to run the operation. The rusted old truck had been there for years and I rebuilt the engine. The fuel tank ran for quite a while since the six-cylinder engine was the old, 1953 'Blue Flame Six' of yesteryear. A simple engine to work on when needed—a kudos for Chevy.

Susan's forté was decorating all the rooms. The day after Thanksgiving was the day to pack away the entire pilgrim, turkey, pumpkin and other accents from turkey day and return them to the already overfilled attic. Each corner of the upper level had boxes of decorations that she stored for various occasions. Christmas had the most, but Valentine's Day, the Fourth of July, and Easter and maybe Memorial Day, ran a close second. Each box contained the decorations for special occasions and was labeled by room; hence the living room and den had the largest accumulation of artifacts old and new, figurines and trinkets that were destined to be displayed periodically.

My office and library were in the back of the house. It was originally a smaller room that once provided an access conduit direct to a barn that was now long gone. It burned years earlier. I required few 'decorations' in my little *escape* from reality. My room was for listening to music in a recliner or writing the next novel. It was quiet back there and dark. It set the mood for inspiration and also had a grand view of the backyard birds and wildlife—the occasional stray moose entertained me but so did raccoons and frequent white-tailed deer that sought our apples left over from fall. The back of the house faced south so the winter sun provided some heat and reduced the wood needed for the wood stove or the need for oil in the main house.

With the home in Washington ready for the holidays two days after Thanksgiving, the acquisition of a tree was the only chore left in completing the final décor. We still had a few days before his birthday. The date was close to mine. Good conjugal timing on the part of Susan and me. It was no wonder that, with the home set for Christmas and the New Year, she would have concern over my hair-brained idea to celebrate Christmas in a new/old memory in the North End of Boston. We hadn't even purchased the house as yet in Little Italy and she was already showing trepidation for herself and Grazie's reaction to the idea. Both birthdays would be low key, but we'd celebrate with a dinner in Boston.

"Honey. Why now?" she asked, exasperated.

I was quick to immediately point out that 'this was an opportunity of a lifetime, *my* lifetime.' The home would never be available again and financially we were in a position to handle it.

"We aren't moving there permanently," I reiterated softly, "we will use it for some holidays and for weekend jaunts to Boston in spring and summer." I padded my case with the opportunities 'for her' to have time away, to go shopping in a major city when she wanted, eat ethic food of our heritage, my heritage, and see the historic sites and sports events with our son. 'He' would have access to his beloved Red Sox and the popular players were within reach for autographs, especially behind the Fenway dugout, I insisted, as opportunistic enticements of rare fortune.

She was more concerned about displacing her son's love of our Cape home at Christmas, not to mention her own happiness with the surroundings and low-key Christmas holidays in the woods. Financially, she knew we could do it. My recent good fortune with a publisher of note and a good chance at Hollywood movies from my creative exposé, made my case even more plausible.

"How will Grazie accept this?" she asked, with chagrin. "He's used to Christmas *here* at home. He knows Santa will come down that chimney in our living room. This may be his last year of fantasy and I want him to enjoy the moment. There won't be that chimney and hearth, and 200-year-old timber mantle from our barn . . . in the North End," she offered, in a sensible and courteous argumentative style. She lay back and tossed her blonde hair behind her face with one hand. *How could I argue with her points of reason?* She was nude and beautiful. *Was I being selfish or fortuitous in my haste and plan?*

For a moment I hesitated and sighed in a sympathetic quandary. She made sense and I was being foolish. Then I had a brainwave like no other.

"La Chiave di Natale," I said, in rapid fashion. She looked perplexed and insulted.

"John, are you swearing at me in Italian?" she asked, sitting up and covering her breasts in defiance. They were off limits now.

"No, Love, not even close," I retorted, grabbing her hand softly to kiss. "It's Italian for *The Christmas Key*."

"What are you talking about?" she asked, with apprehension, "what Christmas key?"

It was at that point that I needed to explain the tradition in the North End when one does not have a fireplace and a chimney in their home—one for Santa to come down. By the end of my explanation, she was rethinking the matter and coming over to my side, both mentally and physically.

"But we've decorated this home already and Grazie thinks we'll be here for the holidays."

I explained that when he came home from school the next day I would take him cross country skiing in the back forty and bounce the idea off him, over a campfire by the nearby stream and waterfall. As far as I was concerned, his opinion was a valid as ours and his concerns would need to be considered, even as an eight-year-old.

"Oh, one more thing," she shared with raised eyebrows and concern, "with Christmas right around the corner, how can I possibly decorate a home that we don't even own yet?" Valid point!

"I can call the Realtor in the morning and discuss with her the concerns and any other paperwork needed for the *formal* signed offer. I can now seal the deal and fax her. I'm sure she'll get back to us as soon as possible. The owners live in Florida in the winter. They may be able to rent the place to us in the interim, if we agree in principle to buy it."

Susan lay back down, somewhat in concert with the idea. She leaned against my chest and kissed my neck. "You've obviously thought this out well. Did you actually attend the conference or hang out in the North End all the days of the trip?"

"Did both, My Love."

"You obviously want this very badly, don't you? I can see it in your eyes. It's the same look that you gave me when you proposed to me. You wanted me just as badly, foolish man." She smiled and sat on top of me. The conversation was over for the moment and she needed time to think.

She, or should I say *we,* had desired a second child for a year or so. I was not one to hold back the effort. The North End desire on my part was not as intense as my desire to make love at that very moment. We were in symphony with the movement and I had the rest of the night to plan the detailed issues for Elena in Boston.

Right now, all I wanted was Susan.

Chapter 10

Graziano, my little 'Grazie,' arrived home at 2:15 P.M. He stumbled in the door and was fatigued by the backpack loaded with books, snacks uneaten and homework for the night. I had been writing all day on my computer. The new novel was to be, *The Christmas Key.* That was the *working draft* title. In the end, I might use the same title in Italian. I couldn't decide and that didn't matter at this point. The draft could have any name at this juncture of its infancy.

His mother had baked cookies for him and the whole house smelled of cinnamon and brown sugar. *Would we be able to match that magic in Boston?* I wondered. I was convinced that it was doable since any kitchen, old or new, could smell like that during the holidays.

After a period of relaxation and us sitting around the pine table with cookies and milk while talking of his day at school, I was ready to offer him the trip through the woods. I had already packed hot dogs, chips and other goodies to entice him. The idea of a fire near the waterfall and bubbling stream, with hot dogs and adventure, won him over. To my surprise he was quick to agree to the trip. I must admit that I was nervous and was hopeful that he would understand our dilemma, the one his mother and father now had.

* * *

Cooking hotdogs over an open fire in winter, when you can cook them *indoors*, may seem foolish. Both Grazie and I cross-country skied (with snowshoes on our backs) to the woods behind the house. We had limited light and time for the adventure, since New England experienced shorter days of light in winter. We wanted to be home by 4:30 P.M. and daylight would be reduced by then.

The reason for two means of transportation is a lesson learned in my high school and later college days when I went cross-country skiing and unexpectedly broke a ski tip. The trip home was miserable, and to this day, I have always taken the light aluminum snowshoes with me on all trips. It's a backup plan and a wise one. In high school, I was on a ski team and competed in Nordic events. Cross-country was one event and ski jumping was the other one. The jumping competitions were at ski areas and state forest facilities. We ski-jumped 30- and 40-meter hills in competition, and those airborne experiences were uneventful most times. I crashed once and hurt one leg seriously. Normally the ski comes off when you fall—this one didn't and I followed the ski, not it following *me,* in a series of helicopter turns down the outrun like a rag doll.

Standing atop the jump hill and above the lip was enough to make your heart race and for anxiety to set in. I can remember kids peeing at the top, in fear. The classic yellow holes in the snow were numerous.

I could hear the stream bubbling a few short minutes into the woods. We had less than one-quarter mile to our summertime open area where we had chained a picnic table to a tree. It was located near the small falls that were ten feet high. With a warmer temperature today, the stream was flowing freely circumventing and bending around the rocks and snow-capped branches and limbs. It was as pretty in snow as it was in summer. The table was still there but someone had worked on it a bit. They removed one leg for firewood. The trek through the pines was easy since we had cleared a trail in fall after the bugs were gone. It was an annual event to maintain the path to paradise.

The fire pit stuck out of the snow since the recent storm had not covered all of the circular rocks, which I had assembled months earlier. I sent Grazie on a mission to find some dry bows, old pine branches near the bottom of trees and a pinecone or two. Pinecones are great starter fuel and loaded with pinesap. I had matches in my pocket sealed dry in a Ziploc bag for emergencies.

In short time, the fire was blazing and we were laughing and telling stories while roasting hotdogs on sticks that had been shaved to a sharp point with my Swiss Army knife. They are part of the emergency provisions and I carry one or two, when in the woods.

"How was school today?" I asked him, getting more serious. "Did your homework get turned in?"

"Yes," he replied, proudly, "got an 'A' on a quiz too."

"Good," I said. "You've done well this winter and that means that the better you do in school, the more often we can get away to ski or snowboard in New Hampshire or Vermont." He was pleased that I was paying him some positive vibes.

I managed to converse a few minutes as we ate the dogs and snacked on trail mix and chips. We had hot chocolate, which I carried in my backpack. He was unaware of that and loved the surprise. That was my cue to bring up the North End matter.

"I was in Boston as ya know this week and saw a nice apartment/condo in my old neighborhood in the North End." He sat quietly looking at the fire and watching the flames dance among the twigs of pine. He threw in an occasional pinecone, which flared up from the pine oil.

"Are we moving, Dad?" he asked, straight away. He stopped eating and looked at me with his big brown eyes. I was in a panic for he was way too quick to respond.

"No Son, we're not moving. We love our house here and this nice brook and the woods."

"Good," he reacted and then started chewing again. He blew on the smoking hotdog that he had cooked.

"How would you feel if we had two homes, one fulltime and one for fun?" I baited him. The reaction was immediate.

"Sure . . . why not?"

"Well, we have a chance to buy the house I grew up in. It's for sale and I saw it again yesterday. Wouldn't that be cool?"

He smirked and said, "As long as we keep this one we have. I like the holidays here."

I was on a slippery slope now since my intent was to spend some holidays in Boston and he was unaware of my plans.

"Holidays, like Christmas, can be fun there as well," I iterated. "I had a lot of fun there as a child your age. There are lights and festivals and great things to do around Christmas. There's even an indoor skating rink by the harbor in the North End. It's near the Charlestown Bridge. I think they keep it open year round as well." He seemed shocked since there was only a temporary place to skate in one park in Washington. The Boston rink appealed to him since the local rink was bumpy and crusty from snow and the infrequent plowing and watering to keep it smooth. It relied on volunteers, not like a paid staff in Boston.

"Sounds good," he responded and I was beginning to feel a bit better. I knew I was winning when he asked if we could do Christmas there this year.

"Yes . . . possibly but I need your input, your approval. Mom and I think it's a cool idea but we needed your consent. Your vote means a lot to us."

"No problem, Dad, but my friends are all here."

"You can invite them to Boston for weekends," I suggested. "They may not want to come home if they eat those cookies and cannolis from Mike's." I explained that Mike's was a great pastry shop.

"Yummy," he added.

He seemed even more anxious for me to pursue the home in the North End. As we chatted, he changed the subject two or three times. At last, I suggested we begin heading home. The sun had dipped below the lowest pine and the temperature was dropping. There was still light, but not much left.

We quickly snuffed out the fire with water from the brook and then covered it in snow. A small amount of steam continued to vent but there was no smoke.

The ski home was uneventful and I was proud of him for discussing the matter of the second home without crying or becoming sad. In less than twenty minutes, we were at the backdoor. I put away the equipment in the shed and he headed into the house to see his mother. Dinner was ready and we were full of dogs and chips. Mother understood and suggested we eat later, around seven. For hours that night I thought of Grazie's maturity at his tender age. That experience would become a Chapter in my new novel. I quickly went to my writing room and library and jotted down notes about the experience at the waterfall. I could fashion a plot from those notes. They were gentle reminders of a fine day in my adult life, a special closeness with my son. I thought of my father.

When Grazie went to the bathroom, his mother approached me for a hug.

"How'd the bonding go?" she asked, expecting a long story.

I hugged her tightly and whispered in her ear, "Piece of cake, Baby . . . piece of cake."

Chapter 11

Susan was busy preparing Graziano for school the next morning. I was on the phone with Elena at 8:30 discussing an offer on the North End property. It was clear that a reasonable offer might seal the deal. She worked for the seller but wanted the deal to culminate for all parties involved. Her commission would be large at seven percent. I wanted the house and the seller wanted to stop paying taxes on property at which they didn't spend much time.

"I think that my initial offer should be in the $500K plus range," I told Elena. She was hesitant to respond and then said, "Low or high $500s?"

"I was thinking $549K. Might that work?"

"I can present that to them and I am required to make that offer known to them but I think they will turn down something that low," she advised. "They had a prior offer a month ago that was $500K and they passed it up."

"Look," I said candidly, "we are not buying the whole complex, merely the apartment or condo that once sold for peanuts when my dad owned it. The old building will take renovation and no apartment in that structure is worth what they are asking. The price seems inflated for that part of the North End. It's not like we will have a view of Boston Harbor," I argued casually.

"True," Elena said, "it's not a room with a view unless you strain to see the North Church. I can only advise you that other deals were turned down when the seller felt the offers were 'lowballing.' They have money and can afford to wait for the right buyer."

I went quiet for a minute. I had to think how I could manipulate this deal and be appealing.

"Look Elena, you know we want the place. It was my boyhood home. No one else would appreciate it more than us. Perhaps you can tell the sellers that."

"Okay John, I will do what I can and get right back to you. They are supposed to call me at 10 A.M. They may want a higher deposit to insure the deal and to test your sincerity. You originally wanted to put $30K down, but I would recommend $50K to sweeten the pot. How does that sound?"

"Okay, I guess. Let's write up $549K and $50K *down* and fax it to them. If you draft it this morning, please fax a copy to me for our signature. It will be our letter of intention and an act of good faith. I can fax it back to you for forwarding."

Elena FaFauci was happy to move things forward and to get her assistant to work up the papers back at the office. I was now fatigued from the conversation and said goodbye and good luck. I moved from the couch in my library, to a nearby recliner. In moments, I intermittently dozed off. Real estate deals were not my bag. I hated the bureaucracy and the games that people played. It was simple business—the sellers wanted to sell places for more than they were worth and the buyers wanted to get the properties for nothing. In between the principals and us were the Realtors who wanted the deal completed and a fat commission check at closing. It was all bull-ticky.

Susan had gone to Graziano's school to volunteer in a classroom. I would rest in the supple, leather chair until Elena called me back. The chair had a built in vibrator and heater unit and I turned both on. The $1200 recliner was the best out there—the famed one that Brookstone or a Sharper Image sold.

I was tired and in no real mood to write another few pages in my manuscript, therefore I fell asleep during some morning game shows on TV. The time flew by and the next thing I heard was the phone ringing. It was just after 10 A.M.

Chapter 12

I hadn't mentioned the 'Christmas Key' to my son in our discussions. I didn't want to tell him that the condo had no fireplace or chimney for Santa. The *Chiave* would be a surprise and hopefully would work.

The night of the hotdog event in the woods, I sat with Susan at the pine table in the kitchen and sorted through some Christmas boxes that were from my dad's home. I was curious to see if 'the Key' from my youth and other objects of the holidays could be located. It was *one more* attempt by me to find it among his belongings.

Grazie was busy and intensely watching *The Polar Express*, albeit early in December. I was fond of the original book, which we had given him a few years earlier but the movie with Tom Hanks was the best ever produced. Far and away, the book and movie illustrations, story and commercially produced DVD were exceptional productions. The message of the book was a clear signal that a simple sleigh bell could restore the faith in Santa and the spirit of the holidays. It, in my mind, will be a classic forever. Grazie loved the movie and the train to the North Pole. He actually believed that the movie was real. To most children and adults, it is. To those without the holiday spirit and fantasy, it isn't.

I had wished that *I* had written *that* book. I always felt that Christmas was a time of year when people loved one another and rid themselves of the hatred and animosity in the world. The lyrics, *Why can't we have Christmas the whole year around,* from the tune, *We Wish You a Merry Christmas,* should be a national anthem.

The box from my father's home contained no remnants of the decorations like the tree top angel or *La Chiave di Natale*—the key to the front door. I was saddened that they were no longer around or even in his former possession. Why were they missing?

We rifled though other items, old strings of lights that were so ancient that the wires were stiff and the pointed and fluted bulbs of the day were losing their surface paint. I plugged in one set and it failed to light. I would play with it later. Back then, the lights were destined to go off or not light completely if one bulb was burned out, loose or missing. The serial type wires shut the whole thing down—unlike today, where they are wired a bit differently; one bad bulb doesn't turn off the whole line of lights. The old light sets were memorable anyway.

The box also contained some ornaments that were old and of value. During the WWII years, many ornaments were probably produced in countries other than at home in the United States. A whole tin of glass ornaments, unique and beautiful, appeared to be handcrafted. I saw no mark for a country but they resembled the artistic style of glass-beaded work typical of Italy or the Philippines. There were some twelve or so ornaments accompanied by glass-beaded red, felt balls that were football shaped. We studied the glass ornaments closely. Some were fragile and had what appeared to be fruit emblazed on a silver background of painted glass. Susan studied each piece, holding them up to the light for even more appreciation. I strained to remember the ornaments that my father had saved for posterity. For all we knew, they had been purchased at a small shop in the North End. The glass ones looked familiar to me, but the felt Christmas balls were not. Each was beautiful in its own right.

"These are gorgeous, Honey," she commented, "I've never seen the likes of them before—how beautiful."

"Amazing that they have survived all these years," I commented, holding one hexagon up to the ceiling light. It shimmered even after decades of being stored in attics or cellars. "They seem familiar to me but I'm not sure at what age I would have been when dad put them on our tree."

"The box has a note, Honey—written in pencil." Susan studied the faint writing on the dust covered ornament box. "It reads, 'To My Love at Christmas—your wife, Maria.'" The date of the note preceded my birth so it was clear that my mother had given them to my father before a forthcoming Christmas and my emergence into the world. Perhaps she was *with child* then.

I never saw them on his Christmas trees in the last years of his life. Perhaps they were too sad a reminder for him to hang in the home each year.

"Let's hang them in Boston," she voiced to me in a powerful statement. I smiled and nodded. She was committing to the new abode before we even owned it. "We can buy a small tree and hang these few items on the branches. It will be a personal tree in Grazie's room."

"I think ya have a plan, dear." I was amazed at her thoughtfulness and longing for the North End property. Those were positive future ideas and music to my ears.

The missing 'angel' that I remembered atop our tree each year was stunning. It was a porcelain figure and face, covered with silk and ribbons of crimson and gold. Her wings were made of finely suspended lace and fragile. Underneath her dress was an inverted, fiberboard cone that allowed us to place her high on the peak branch in the center of the tree. She always sat there illuminated by three or four nearby lights on the string. We changed the red or green bulbs to yellow or white so she was always in view.

In a separate, medium-sized cardboard box was a Nativity scene— individual pieces and figurines handmade in Italy. There was the Madonna, Joseph and the baby Jesus. Additionally, there were two or three animals: camels, cows and sheep. The Three Wise Men were hand-painted, complete with gold urns in their hands—gifts of incense for the newborn Christ child.

The stable of wood I remember was handcrafted by my father. He used scrap wood to make the roof and walls and side rails. Gray cedar shingles were used for the walls, the back and roof of the building and hand split to be fashioned into the siding of the building. The manger was of porcelain and laden with straw from many previous Christmases. The straw bedding was old but cushioned the infant in the crib. I felt a bit emotional and had to get a glass of water from the kitchen as an excuse. All the memories of my younger days with my father at Christmastime replayed in my mind like a movie of old.

Susan was perceptive. "Let's finish this another day," she offered, sensing my quiet thoughts. "We've plenty of time to sort through these wonderful holiday decorations."

We watched the movie with our son and focused on his laughter. Christmas was for children and his exuberance showed its true meaning.

*   *   *

It took another day for Elena to get back to us regarding our offer on the property. We had to fax *more* paperwork to the seller to review. The usual lead paint and radon disclaimers, etc. When she did get in touch she apologized for the delay. She had three other closings and the owners of the Prince Street property were on an apparent cruise from Miami to the Bahamas. The cruise was about sixty miles from port-to-port. While at sea, the ability to reach the sellers by cell phone was 'limited—to nonexistent.' Both Susan and I accepted the excuse as reasonable.

Although anxiety had set in for me during those extra hours, I had relegated myself to accept the fact that the deal might not go through. Elena had warned us that the owners rejected previous offers on the property. What was clear to me was that if it were meant to be, 'it would happen.' Elena had indicated that she thought our offer would be given strong consideration. We were encouraged by her comments. She knew the seller's well and had the inside track on the deal. Elena had much invested in the agreement. The commission would be lucrative and welcomed just before Christmas. When she finally had news, both Susan and I got on the house phones together. One was in the kitchen and the other in the living room. Neither one was cordless so we chatted from two separate rooms.

"I have good news and bad," she relayed to us.

"Like what? What bad news?" I said, defensively.

"The owners are interested in your offer but they can't close until after New Years, and if I recall, you wanted to be in there, before Christmas."

I was pleasantly shocked by the good news of them verbally accepting our offer but was afraid that the owners might want to return to Boston for the Christmas holidays and festivities.

"Do they have plans for the condo for the holidays?" I asked, with remorse.

"No. No. That's not the issue. They're traveling and will be in the Bahamas and maybe on another island for Christmas. They don't envision being back here until after the First of the Year. They do *want* to be at the closing if all is agreed upon."

I sighed with relief for that left the possibility that we might be able to occupy the residence, even temporarily, for a few days over the Christmas week.

"Is there no way that it can't be accomplished by say, a *power of attorney?*" I asked. It seemed logical and Susan peered around the corner of her room while nodding in agreement. She said nothing on the phone.

"In this case, that won't work. The owners wish to meet the new tenants in person. I tried to have them handle the closing through their lawyer but they insisted on being here when the right deal is consummated."

"Can you ask them if we may stay there over the holidays, perhaps three or four days, or possibly rent it for the week? We were hoping to experience the North End with our son and partake of any festivals nearby."

"I mentioned that to them and they were graciously willing to let you do that *gratis* should they receive the signed contractual agreement of intent and the deposit of $50K. Basically, the P&S, a deposit and any additional conditions for closure would need to be in order and received by them."

I was pleased to hear that they would allow us the use of the condo for free. That was unexpected.

"That's kind of them, Elena. We surely can get the money and final paperwork in order as soon as possible. They had the draft offer already correct, the P&S that we faxed?"

"Yes," she replied. "You'll need to get me the bank check and all should be in order. We can then arrange for the lawyers and the principals to meet at my office and select a firm convenient date for January. Does that sound okay?" Both Susan and I said, yes, at the same time. Elena and Susan chatted for a bit since they had never met.

"One more thing," I interjected. "We're coming to Boston as a family this weekend and we're hoping to have Susan and son, Graziano see the condo. Can that be arranged?"

"Surely," she replied. "I'll be around. Just call me once you're in town. Where will you be staying?"

"We are booked into the Marriott near Christopher Columbus Park," I advised.

"Good," she offered. "That's close by, a short walk, and perhaps I can treat you all to lunch at Artu."

"That'd be very nice," Susan and I responded, almost simultaneously. We often thought alike.

"It's nearby the condo actually and a nice quaint restaurant with the best 'chicken Marsala' in town."

"I'm game," I replied. "I passed the restaurant in my travels earlier in the week and the setting looked inviting and casual, unpretentious to be precise."

"Excellent," Elena responded, cordially. "See you this weekend on Saturday."

We all agreed that the lunch would be best on that particular day. We wanted to spend time with Grazie at either the Museum of Science or at the New England Aquarium. The aquarium was next to the hotel and the science museum a short cab ride to Cambridge, near Memorial Drive. It was doubtful that we could visit two venues in one day. Grazie would get to pick the venue and Susan would make time to shop at the stores near Faneuil Hall the next day.

After the call, Susan came in to hug me. "Congrats, My Love, you'll be buying your boyhood home. They've accepted our offer—in principle."

"I'm shocked at the whole thing," I replied, while holding her tightly. "You and I can begin to add to the family there—the romantic North End."

"Really," she said, smugly, and with a cautious smile.

"I'm already pregnant," she volunteered, shrugging her shoulders, nonchalantly.

"What?" I was taken aback, but thrilled at the news.

"Yup . . . found out today . . . you're going to be a dad again!"

"Wonderful. What a nice Christmas gift. I love you."

"Me too. I couldn't be happier." We embraced for a solid minute.

Both of us were tired from the call, the anxiety of the coming holidays and now . . . the news of the pregnancy. We had to get organized and rapidly. We were going to Boston in three days. Susan and I sat on the couch and said little. We merely snuggled closely and appreciated the fact of how lucky we were. Our son would be home soon from school. He knew nothing of the forthcoming trip, the purchase of the condo or the fact that he was to be a brother. All in all, it was a beautiful day and life was good.

Chapter 13

The visit with Aldo, Jr. at his North End shoe and leather shop sparked a renewed interest by me in knowing the whereabouts of Dominick Russo. He was as close to me as Aldo. Like most kids with dreams of exciting jobs when they grow up, Dom always wanted to be a fireman. It seemed that 'becoming a fireman' was the choice of most boys that I knew; girls wanted to become veterinarians. Not much has changed these days, as I understand it. Boys still like 'red' trucks and girls love animals.

I didn't burden Aldo, Jr. about the whereabouts of Dom when we first met. I was on a mission to find Aldo, Sr., my closest friend. I did and that was traumatic enough—a victim of a war that was disputed by many and brought pain to the USA in the 1960s and beyond, for almost a decade (1965-1973). I didn't know if Dom was a veteran as well, or if he had moved away after high school. He always talked about his relatives in New York's 'Little Italy' or those in a town called Raritan, New Jersey. I had been to both towns on trips for book signings but never thought to seek out the Russo name. There were *many* Russo's in NYC. It would have been cumbersome and maybe even futile. The fact was I had no clue where he might have settled anyway. If possible, during the forthcoming weekend in Boston, I would try to revisit Dom's old neighborhood or revisit Aldo, Jr.'s shop to seek the whereabouts of Dominick or his family.

Dominick always remained large in stature, even in high school and I suspect that he would have had health issues if he didn't lose weight as an adult. It was possible that he 'passed on' like Aldo did. Then again, who would know if he became modern-day trim with the diet and exercise craze, was married or had five or ten kids? It was a personal challenge that I wanted to pursue in Boston.

*   *   *

Susan, Grazie and I arrived at the Marriott by Boston Harbor on Friday afternoon. The valet service parked our SUV and we quickly registered for a room overlooking the water. We lucked out in that we were upgraded to a suite on the side facing Logan Airport and the wharves north and south of the busy commercial waterway. The hotel had a cancellation and was somehow alerted to the fact that I had been written up in the Globe after the writer's conference, cited as a promising author from Western Massachusetts. *My, how they were confusing me with well-known writers,* I thought. I relished in the moment anyway—fifteen minutes of fame. Ego boost or not, I accepted the kudos.

Pulling back the lace curtains in the multiple windows revealed a panoramic view from the Mystic-Tobin Bridge to the South Boston Gas Tank of famed multi-colored paint. There were originally two rainbow-like tanks and Grazie was excited about the wonderfulness of the Disney-like colors especially against the blanket of the recent snow.

Historically, in 1971, Boston Gas commissioned artist, Corita Kent to paint the tanks. The large canvas-like artwork is acclaimed to be the world's largest copyrighted piece of art. Grazie focused on the one remaining landmark left, since the other had been torn down in recent years.

He claimed to see a face in the design. I told him it was possible but that, to me, it resembled a rainbow.

The original art, I seemed to remember, was controversial since the artist, Kent, was active in protesting the Vietnam War of the 60s and 70s. The Dorchester tanks were a brilliant, permanent billboard off Route 93 South and the controversial blue stripe was surmised to be the bearded image of Ho Chi Minh. People had suggested that the man's profile was unmistakably the leader in Vietnam. The gas company refuted that claim and suggested that it was a coincidence. They denied that the artist painted the image of Minh, intentionally. Kent has since died and the gas company had the art repainted on the only remaining tank. The profile of a man is less distinct in the new art form, but still there.

The harbor landings and docks, that normally look a bit dismal or dirty, were covered with a white sheet of snow that was pristine and appealing to visitors. Our son stood at the glass windows and watched as large tankers approached from the south end of the Boston Harbor entrance and outer islands. Even in winter and at dusk, harbor cruise ships took sightseers out for dinner cruises and special function parties, mostly corporate holiday parties and get-togethers at this time of year.

The boats departed from the wharf near the hotel entrance. The New England Aquarium was on the other side, in direct opposition to the hotel's front doors. Everything was conveniently located for the weekend and a quick walk to nearby Christopher Columbus Park, many restaurants and the North End's expanse of one-square-mile. Faneuil Hall Marketplace was a stone's throw away to the west.

"Can we see the statue of Paul Revere?" Grazie asked, with excitement. "How about cookies at the pastry shop you mentioned," he yelled, with a broad grin.

"Tomorrow, Son," I replied, patting his head. "We'll have lots of time tomorrow."

Susan seemed to concur that we would see all the sights and the aquarium over the next two days. She was hungry and I suggested that we grab dinner at the Union Oyster House, one of her favorite spots for seafood, and a noted Boston landmark. It was billed as the oldest, continuously operating restaurant in the United States. Even JFK ate in a favorite booth on the second level. Oysters, lobsters and clams were a specialty and Graziano was willing to tackle a 1½-pounder himself. We had taught him well, even in the woods of Washington, Massachusetts.

The next day would entail taking the family out early to see the condo, our new second home, to be. Lunch with Elena would follow. We were anxious to get the real estate deal settled with Elena and have Susan and Graziano pleasantly in concert with the acquisition and life-changing decision. It was my home at one point in my life, but would they embrace the same attraction and determination that I had, to acquire it? Had they been more pragmatic in their final analyses?

Saturday couldn't come fast enough for me.

Chapter 14

The meal was wonderful at the Union Oyster House and the white lights of the nearby Faneuil Hall complex and the Old State House made the whole Quincy Market area festive. We left the restaurant and walked past the well-lit stores that were now closed for the day. They would reopen on Saturday morning.

Boston was remarkable at night during the holidays. It was more than 'historic' and the Freedom Trail, now covered with snow or slush, outlined the sidewalks and paths to history. It was the place to be at Christmas for families. Adults and kids had all the tourist attractions at their disposal. The only venues remaining open at this late hour were the Irish bars, cafes and a nearby McDonalds. Two or three well-known restaurants were open as well. The Food Court in Quincy Market was closed for the evening and workers were cleaning their service booths and food prep areas. A garbage truck appeared late to clear the areas behind the buildings of trash. There were less fruit vendors than in summer when the area bustled with customers. In winter, only one or two diehards sold produce. Most waited until spring.

Grazie wanted to see the lights in the North End. He loved the red, green and white strings of holiday lights that ran down Hanover. We did as well, as Susan placed her arm in mine for a slow stroll down the famed street. People were still milling around and the older men stopped to stare at my beautiful wife, an obvious 'tourist / visitor' with long blonde hair. The occasional cat whistle was complimentary to her. She felt special. I shook my finger at one old man, in jest. He smiled at being caught with wandering eyes.

"Mi scusi," he offered, in apology. It didn't matter; men were staring at her from all directions.

"I just love this place, Honey," she commented. "This could be the best idea you've had . . . since marrying me," she teased, with a chuckle.

"For sure," I replied, keeping my eyes on the horny Italian men commenting in their native language. "You have a lot of eyes on you here. Are you sure that you'll be able to handle the compliments of the neighborhood?"

"I think it'll be easy . . . and flattering. All men are the same—'when they unzip their pants, their *brains* fall out,'" she stated, unequivocally. I laughed at her wit. Grazie looked confused.

"Never mind, Son," I offered.

I chuckled even harder since that type of comment was not typical of my wife. Graziano was not sure what to make of the comment. He just shook his head in dismay—innocent confusion.

It was getting late and we grew tired of Grazie's begging. We stopped briefly at Mike's for a pastry and cookie or two. The young lad was happy to see the appetizing variety in front of him, all the display cases were illuminated and overflowing with choices—selections with jimmies, whipped cream or shaved chocolate. He couldn't settle on the lemon, anise or a chocolate assortment so we decided to get two pounds of everything that he pointed too.

The smells were incredible. Our selection was boxed and then tied with string in a manner so fast that the woman serving us had her hands flying left and right. The string came off a spool on the ceiling; it spun like a top.

Thinking back to my boyhood life, I remembered the local butcher, Mr. Renzi, performing the same motion. He wrapped the fresh cuts of meat in white paper and closed the package like a Christmas present.

String held the top and sides together on the cookie box. It made a nice handle for carrying the treats to the hotel. A pastry chef gave Grazie a complimentary cookie for the walk.

That was the ambiance of Mike's Pastry Shop. Half the fun was watching the lines of people selecting the cholesterol, and fat-laden, ricotta and sugar delicacies. Each one seemed to be a million calories per bite. A woman stuffed cannolis and crème horns by hand, using a 'pastry bag' and right in front of us. She dusted the cannolis with confectioner's sugar as a finale.

We left the shop with our mouths watering and knew that Saturday would require another visit to Hanover to compare the nearby 'Modern' pastry shop with Mike's noted creations.

Our son was tired and we needed to walk back to the hotel. We found our way to Richmond Street and crossed by Christopher Columbus Park.

Susan was tired as well. Having recently confirmed her own pregnancy with a pharmacy pregnancy test, fatigue was sitting in even in the earliest stages of her gestational state. I too was happy to get back to the room. The huge bed was room enough for all three of us to spread out. Morning would come fast and we had an early meeting with Elena. I was overly anxious to show the condo to Susan and Graziano.

In less than fifteen minutes after arriving at the hotel, all three of us were sound asleep.

Chapter 15

I sleep quite lightly when on the road. A least two times during the night I was awakened by people returning to their rooms on our floor. One couple was laughing and loud, but innocuous. They quickly disappeared into a nearby room. A bunch of revelers seemed to be arriving home from a holiday party. They'd consumed a large quantity of booze, I surmised. The negotiation of the hallway seemed difficult for them. Fortunately for us, they all ended up in another suite at the end of the hall.

I was afraid that Grazie might awaken from the raucous hotel guests but he never budged. I was the one who now had insomnia. I tried to read a newspaper in a chair at the far end of the suite but soon became inspired to fabricate a Chapter for the next novel that I had started. I opened the laptop on a nearby desk designed for the business traveler (with free Internet) and began to type a fictional scenario based around our evening's experiences at the restaurant, Faneuil Hall and the Hanover Street pastry shop. The visions of the night were fresh in my mind. If there were to be a 'dialogue' in the new contrived paragraphs, I would add most of the characters and conversations later. Half of the text in novels is descriptive exposé, i.e. people, places, things or events. It was nearly midnight when I came to the realization that I was tired. I was typing poorly and misspelling words. The 'grammar check' program on the laptop showed me leaving out verbs and capitalizing the wrong words. Those 'slips' made me shut the computer down and return to bed.

* * *

A wakeup call at 7 A.M. startled me. Susan and Grazie seemed not to stir. By now, the sun was rising in the east and the cold winter air created a stunning sunrise of reds, oranges and lavender. Cirrus clouds streaked above Logan Airport. I pulled back the curtain just enough to watch the sun elevate over the horizon and then located the coffee pot on a table near the kitchenette. The hotel suite was large with lush carpet and offered most amenities that one would desire. The bathroom contained an anteroom and dresser for women with Hollywood-like lighting for makeup application and a shower that was black marble tiled with gold-filigreed fixtures that looked and 'smelled' expensive.

The coffee pot had those round filters that made about four, four ounce cups of *instant brewed* coffee. I was able to find the sweetener and powered creamer enough to get me by until we went to breakfast. A newspaper lay outside the door and I read the Globe while my family slept. We would grab a *real* breakfast when they awoke.

I have always been lucky. Lucky in business, lucky in love, especially now, and lucky to have a family that nurtured and fostered my desire to be a writer. They knew it came easy and fast for me and left me alone when the creative juices were flowing. I never seemed to have writer's block, and if left uninterrupted, I could usually pen a novel in three months. The draft would then be reworked over another month or two, and subsequently edited for errors.

The one thing that kept the new novel flowing was the occasional flashback to my days in elementary, junior high and high school. It was surprising to me that the recent two trips to Boston's North End, including this one, stimulated the fond memories that I had with relatives and my father. My nearest relatives were like my 'foster mothers,' especially my aunts on both sides. Two in particular, Aunt Millie and Aunt Connie were close to me. Both were of Italian descent but Aunt Connie was more 'Old World.' She made the best Italian cookies and pizzelles. The pizzelle is the snowflake-like waffle cookie made of flour, eggs, sugar, butter and oil. One uses a pizzelle iron to bake them, one at a time. They are often flavored with vanilla, anise or lemon zest. Italians tout them as one of the 'oldest cookies.' In some parts of Italy, they are known a 'ferratelle.' The region of Abruzzo is where they originated and that happened to also be from where one of my grandparents emigrated. The pizzelle can be served with powdered sugar or rolled when warm and stuffed with a ricotta/ sugar combination typified and used for cannolis. A hazelnut spread is also used on them and Aunt Connie made all versions of the delight.

As kids, we ate them by the dozen, plain or with anise (licorice) and my aunt was the champ of making the best. She was my father's sister and moved to Western Massachusetts like he did. Visits over the Christmas and

Easter holidays always took us to her home, often for feasts and coffee and cookies.

My maternal grandfather made what he called, 'eggnog.' He would take a coffee cup and one egg yolk and add some sugar to the mix. Using a spoon he would stir and beat the mixture until smooth and frothy. He then added black coffee slowly to the cup and gently stirred it. It looked like coffee with cream when he was finished. We all took sips as kids, the neighbor's children and me. To this day, I remember him sitting at the kitchen table in his own apartment in the North End creating this traditional hot drink. This Christmas, I'd share with Graziano the same recipe and hoped it would become a tradition for him when he was older.

My grandfather never told us the name of the drink other than eggnog, but I found a traditional Italian espresso coffee with the same ingredients called Semifreddo, CafeFreddo or Caffe Imperiale (with brandy).

Whatever the name, I sometimes would add anisette to plain black coffee as an adult. The licorice flavor of Sambuca would warm me like a fireplace in a living room. It was called Caffe Royale.

I could hear my wife and son rustling in the bedroom. I had my quiet time writing for a while, but it was time to plan for the busy day—first the visit to the Prince Street home around 9 A.M. and then lunch with Elena at Artu. After that, we hoped to spend the afternoon at the New England Aquarium. The following day, Sunday, would consist of a tour of the North End and a visit to key monuments, nearby markets and shops at Faneuil Hall. In that way, Susan and Grazie could experience and savor a feel for the culture, history and architecture.

Chapter 16

"Nice to meet you both," Elena said, pleasantly, extending her hand to Susan and then to Graziano.

"Hi, John. Let's go upstairs and show your family the property."

We followed Elena, with me being the last to ascend the steps. Susan felt the wall with her hand as if, in her mind, she was feeling what I had touched decades ago as a young boy. The old brass numbers, 76 were still on the door. I saw her sigh briefly and continue up the stairs to the second landing. Elena was quick to open the door to the condo and Grazie ran in to have the first look. For some uncanny reason he managed to stand in front of the living room window that I used to stand in front of as a child. Stepping behind him, I saw what my father had witnessed. He stood looking at the street and people below. It was déjà vu and nostalgic.

"This is so charming," commented Susan, while opening and closing a kitchen cabinet or two, and studying the layout of the bedrooms and living room. I knew she was sight measuring for curtains in her mind, calculating what would fit in cabinets and how any extra furniture we had, might fit. The colors of the walls were not to her liking and she thought deeply on how she would change 'this and that.' Her own taste was far better than the current owners' decor. Susan knew how to stencil walls in the old style, marbleize and wallpaper rooms like a pro. I knew what she was doing and Elena was happy to let us roam room by room at a comfortable pace.

Elena held a clipboard in her hand and a folder full of information on the home under her arm—the North End, the school system and local activities. It was the standard package for new homeowners. The school system information was of lesser value. We had no intention of leaving sleepy little Washington, permanently.

"Well, what do you think?" Elena asked Grazie, who was checking out all the rooms.

"I like it. My dad grew up here. Did ya know that?"

"Yes, Son," she said, "he grew up in that bedroom right over there. Do you think that one will be yours?"

"Oh yes," he boasted. "*That* was dad's room . . . it'll be mine."

Susan and I walked over to the room that Elena had pointed out to Grazie. I saw tears in her eyes—tears of joy and reflection.

"You grew up in that room when you were his age," she said, with appreciation. "*That's* the special room in this house. Who would have known that I would eventually marry the boy from that little blue room?"

"Do you think it's as important as the monuments of history nearby?" I joked.

"To me it is," she said, kissing my cheek softly. I smiled and watched Grazie look in the old closet in that same room. "It'll work," he said, thinking of his clothes and toys.

"I think you'll be happy," said his mother. "I know I'll like the whole place. It's so close to all the good things in Boston. Your Celtics are right around the corner and the Red Sox are a cab ride away, Honey."

"Cool," Grazie said, with exuberance. He was jumping up and down. "Maybe I can meet Varitek."

"What do you think, Dad?" Mom asked. I inferred that 'it was like coming home to a place that had many memories for me.'

Elena jumped into the conversation.

"This is the best sale I've had in years. I have never sold anything in the North End to a *former* resident, not to mention one who *lived here* as a child. I'm excited for you and your family and would like to treat you to lunch. Let's meet up at noon at Artu."

"That'll be great. Let's go, you guys. We've much to see," I recommended. "It's 10 o'clock and we can visit some of the local historical sites before lunch." Susan and Grazie agreed, as we headed for the front door.

We said goodbye to Elena since she had another appointment at 11 A.M. She was smiling and so were we. I had brought the necessary paperwork and a check for the deposit on the Purchase and Sales Agreement. A local bank in Washington had approved our mortgage application, in rapid fashion. The home office was really in the larger city of Pittsfield and I knew the loan officer personally.

The bank had also helped with the expenses needed to have my book screen-written on my own, in the early days of my writing career. Production costs for hardcover printing were costly as well. The bank knew of my impending movie deal for one of my novels. My personal credit was never an issue and in perfect order—I was not a risk.

Elena hugged each of us and soon left in her car. We were to get together shortly and enjoy some authentic Italian food. She didn't want to carry around the large check for the condo deposit and therefore rushed back to the office, before her next appointment.

*   *   *

We spent an hour walking the streets of the North End and near the condo. As it was Saturday morning, I wanted to grab a quick espresso at a local café and then show the family the Paul Revere statue on the horse and his nearby, restored home.

We toured the quaint house, the narrow stairways and rooms of period furniture. Grazie thought of it as a playhouse. It surely looked like one with its meandering rooms and narrow passageways. The basic tour took less than forty-five minutes and Susan found the home charming and well preserved. It gave her ideas for decorations in the condo that we were about to reacquire.

The snow piles were melting from the warm sun and our boots were perfect for the slush that had been created in the early morning. It was nearly lunchtime and we wanted to be sure to get a table at Artu—one that was near the windows so we could observe the people passing by. Elena would meet us there around noon and no prior reservations had been made. She felt it was not needed.

Artu was unpretentious and the fabulous smells of Italian seasonings were enticing. The brick décor began at the front door where the open grill and kitchen were located on the left. A glass case offered many Italian cold salads and antipasti creations. Flames arose from a pan on the grill where a chef was sautéing a dish. The grill was busy.

They were known for their lasagna, chicken Marsala, pasta with red sauce and a variety of roasted vegetables and breads. I was hungry before we were even seated.

Prudie, a waitress who had been there for many years, seated us near a window in the front of the restaurant. The table for four was simple and draped with a red and white-checkered tablecloth. The table rocked slightly due to the uneven brick floor and I was able to fix it with one or two packets of sugar stuffed under a table leg. People began to arrive as if a bell had gone off in the North End. We were lucky to have arrived in time for a table with a view. I checked my wristwatch and Elena was expected to arrive shortly.

*   *   *

My paternal grandfather was quite the gardener. Watching some of the sautéed vegetables arrive at a nearby table made me think of the old gentleman. He came from the 'Old Country' and never had a *real* garden until he moved west of Boston to live with another relative.

Nick was short for Nicola and he was a master at growing the largest vegetables in the smallest spaces. He also raised a few chickens, which he had also done as a child in Italy. The poultry served three purposes: food, eggs and their highly fertile, white byproduct, which smelled just slightly less than pig dung. The secret to his garden flourishing was the last of the three attributes of any chicken production.

As a youngster, we would visit him in spring, and then late summer. By late summer, the vegetables were enormous and proliferating. Plants drooped with large clusters of tomatoes, both the plum and Beefsteak varieties. Carrots were sometimes three to a group and long. Spinach was high and deep green, and peppers, both hot and sweet Bell varieties, were enormous.

I had asked him how he was able to do it. He smiled and showed me a rusted, old fifty-five gallon drum in the backyard, located a few feet from the garden but set in full sun. The top of the barrel had a glass plate covering it. The sun was beaming down on the metal container and I peered over the top in curious fashion. It was near full with water and contained a light green/white layer of scum on the surface. He removed the glass plate and had me take a closer look. The smell was putrid and he chuckled, loudly.

"That's awful, Grandpa," I said, holding my nose with my fingers. "Yuk," I bellowed.

"Atsa nice," he smiled, waving his hand briskly and making believe he enjoyed the aroma. It was perhaps the worst odor that I had ever put my nose next to.

"What's in there?" I asked, nearly nauseated by the experience.

"Chicken shit," he said, clear as a bell. He had no accent on the word, *shit*.

"Poop?" I asked again.

"Yes . . . and acqua-water."

"What's it for?"

"Watcha," he said.

He took a metal ladle with a long handle, a scoop of sorts that a chef would use and moved the scum (foam) on the surface to the inside rim of the barrel. The liquid below was a brown tea-like mixture. He scooped some of the tea into a small, dented kitchen saucepan and then walked me over to the tomato plants. Leaning over and gasping from his heavy weight, he made a ring of the liquid around each plant. He spread the 'tea' a good four inches away from the plant stem, being careful not to touch the leaves.

"*You* do," he said, forcefully, but mentoring like.

I started to spread the liquid methodically and slowly, encircling the base of each plant as he had shown me. He guided my hand away from the healthy plant stems. Because it was acidic, it would harm the plant if the tea were too close.

It was late in the day and the sun was less hot. He took a nearby garden hose from the shed and watered the tomatoes at the base of the plants to rapidly dilute the mixture. He soaked the dirt of each plant. He then placed the glass cover back on the metal drum and said, boasting, "Atsa da secret."

"What secret?" I asked. He told me that the 'tea' was a fermented concoction of water and chicken droppings that had sat for weeks in the bottom of the barrel. He merely replenished the water or added more droppings when low. He used the saucepan to fertilize the garden each week.

I had known for most of my life after that, that chicken poop, pig or mink waste were excellent fertilizer. It was however very caustic and could harm plants or roots of vegetables. It mellowed or seasoned with age and became less acidic. Diluting it in a barrel with water created a nice, natural, liquid fertilizer that was homemade, safe to use and potent. It was still acidic and soaking the plants with water further weakened the caustic potency of the liquid. It made Miracle-Gro looked tame and weak by today's standards.

I was curious and wanted to know what the scum on the top of the water was—it appeared nasty.

"Penicillin," he said, "amold froma da chicken."

"How come?"

"Datsa da secret. When da stuff appears, she's a ready." He pointed to the sun. "She makes it."

He laughed at the frown on my face and we walked back into his house. He knew that the homemade 'tea' grossed me out. On the counter of his old fashioned kitchen were fresh vegetables that we had picked. They were enormous. The zucchinis were three feet long and the tomatoes and carrots were huge. He was preparing a soup with chicken stock and pasta and the veggies from his garden.

I had planned to order minestrone at Artu and knew that the memory of his Saturday vegetable soup would be in the back of my mind. Waxing nostalgic was again taking over my senses.

*　　*　　*

Elena arrived at Artu just as my wife asked me 'where I was.' I appeared deep in thought and was daydreaming. I merely told her that I was thinking of my grandfather.

"You were very far away," she said, concerned. "You okay?" I nodded, yes.

"I was just thinking of his gardens and how he grew things so large."

Elena interrupted the thought.

"I see you all found the place okay," she smiled, sitting immediately next to Graziano.

"May I sit here," she asked, pleasantly.

"Yes, I saved it for you," he said. He was such a charmer at eight-years-old. He would surely be a lady killer when he grew up. "You're quite the gentleman," she offered, and he was embarrassed a bit. "Grazie," he said, smiling . . . trying to impress her even more.

"See, I know Italian," he boasted.

"Siete i benevenuti," she responded, to his thank you—"you're welcome!"

Chapter 17

The bottle of Chianti (Classico Reserve) went rapidly, consumed between Elena and myself. The food at Artu was wonderful. There were plates of shared vegetables, pasta with red sauce and chicken Marsala, a trademark dish of the restaurant. Prudie was a professional waitress, not overbearing or overly attentive, but there when you needed her.

The minestrone was superb and the fried calamari a close second. Elena knew what to order and we became very relaxed around her. She ordered the food in Italian and Prudie appreciated that. They knew each other well. Obviously, Elena had previously brought many clients there, for lunch or for dinner.

I became giddy with the wine. Susan was cute and funny, enjoying the ambiance of the room and the culture of the people in the North End. It was the antithesis of life in Washington, Massachusetts. The North End was unique for her—her first level of comfort was the condo, and now 'the setting' of the restaurant on Prince. It was ironic that our much-anticipated new home and the restaurant were in close proximity, geographically.

The finale was the dessert. They may not all have been baked *on site,* but one wouldn't know that. We shared cannolis, decedent crème puffs, anise-based biscotti and a fruit plate of assorted melons including cantaloupe, honeydew and watermelon. I was stuffed just looking at the delicacies. Graziano sat back against his chair. He was grabbing his stomach in jest, as if full. We knew he had room to try something else.

"Mommy, I'm full. Can we go to the aquarium now?" He was growing impatient with the adult conversation and the overabundance of red wine. We were having too much fun for him and he wasn't directly involved.

"We'll go soon, Son," I offered, to appease him. "There'll be plenty of time, all afternoon. Let's let this wonderful meal settle a bit."

Susan sided with her son like most mothers do. "Honey, we'll leave soon. We need to wait for the bill."

"I'll handle that," offered Elena. "I've got an account here. You three run along and see the fish. Grazie, do you know the Italian word for fish?"

He shook his head, no.

"It's 'pesce.'" She smiled and tapped his shoulder gently. "Enjoy the aquarium and thanks for being so good during lunch."

"Pesce," he repeated. "Let's go see the pesce, Mommy."

We bid farewell to Elena and hugged her before leaving the restaurant. We thanked her profusely for the wonderful meal and I added a few dollars to the tip—a little extra for Prudie.

Within minutes, we were walking the harbor sidewalks to the Marriott and by the harbor cruise kiosks where daily tickets were sold to passengers. The aquarium was in view and Grazie became excited. In the next three hours, we would see every floor and every glass display, including the large tank in the middle, one where the glass at the bottom of the tank was some four inches in thickness.

*   *   *

The New England Aquarium was daunting in size for Grazie. He stood by the mobile sculpture in front of the building. The facility is situated on Central Wharf near Long Wharf and at the end of Milk Street.

Central to the venue is the Great Ocean tank with multiple species of shark, Bonita, turtles and every other common saltwater fish of the Atlantic or Caribbean. The tank serves as a reef where all species cohabitate and circle the cement and glass structure endlessly. Grazie was determined to stand by each of the 52 panels that allowed for varying views of the reef and species. The pressure of the water in the enormous tank was the greatest at the bottom, as one would expect.

Architect Peter Chermayoff designed the tank like many others that he had created around the world. He designed one in Osaka and another in Lisbon. Generally, thick cast acrylic panels (5' X 7') are the viewing rooms. Six hundred species exist in the Boston building and Grazie was determined to see them all. On this particular day, the snow and slush had diminished the attendance by visitors; we were some of the few to see *all* the tanks, large and small.

Graziano had the rare treat of seeing Santa and some elves in the tank.

"Look," he said, excited by the view in front of him. A Scuba diver, complete with a red Santa suit and beard, had entered the tank from the top to feed the fish by hand. Elves in green suits were scrubbing the simulated coral reefs free of debris and algae.

"Amazing," I said to him. "Look over there! A sea turtle is taking the bait from his hand." The turtle was estimated to be at least 100-years-old. Grazie was enchanted by the entire panoramic view and the wondrous display of wildlife from the ocean. It was mesmerizing for all of us.

We moved to other exhibits, including one with a hands-on approach for children. The kids could hold shells, starfish and sea cucumbers, which were slimy and fun for the youngsters.

By late afternoon, we had grown tired of taking in all the sights of the enormous aquarium facilities as well as the informative displays on numerous floors. The 'giant' squid was the most impressive display, second only to the numerous jellyfish, which seemed to dance slowly to chamber music. Their blue hue and undulating patterns, up and down, were fascinating. They were like flowers in the water, akin to sea anemones that waved like flowing wheat fields in the Midwest.

*   *   *

I suggested that we grab a bite to eat for dinner by the wharf. We were hungry and the Boston Sail Loft was a popular restaurant nearby the hotel. I had met Jamie and Phil, the owners, years before during a business lunch. It was fun to see them again and to have the awesome clam chowder that was laced with dill, a nice addition. The owners hadn't previously met my wife or son. They seemed to hit it off from the start.

The first drinks were on them. Again, Susan abstained. Even after having seen fish all day, we ordered the famed fish and chips, which were lightly battered and delicious. The cod was fresh caught and mild. Grazie decided on a hamburger. A fish dinner was now less appealing to him after the day at the aquarium.

Chapter 18

While Susan and Graziano were resting back in the hotel, I went to the lounge for a beer before retiring. The bar area was festive, complete with a Christmas tree and white lights draped everywhere on defoliated birch branches—simulating a small stand of trees in a forest. Snow around the trees was fabricated from cotton that had been stretched out to resemble a flowing landscape. The season was upon us everywhere near the North End and I was anxious for the deal to go down on the condo so we could experience Christmas in our second home. Even with the legal matters delaying the closing on the property, we were assured that we could spend a few days near Christmas at the condo. Susan wanted the place to be as holiday-like as we could imagine. *Festive* was the word she used. Grazie was growing up fast and she wanted him to be a little boy for as long as she could delay it, even if only in her mind.

Susan was already planning a list of items we would need to make Christmas special in the North End.

At the bar, I drank two draft beers in rapid fashion. The Samuel Adams beer was in concert with the history and mood of our weekend. I would have one or two more but got into a conversation with some locals making the mood at the bar even more appealing. I always loved chatting with people, locals or strangers. It fostered and satisfied my curiosity and formulated new fictional characters for my future novels. Authentic character development was critical to all stories of fiction. I usually combined traits of two or more people that I knew, or had met in my life, in order to create the male and female protagonist and antagonist(s). Characters in fiction needed to be realistic in life, ethnicity and in name. A man in a story of the North End would not have the name, Pedro any more that a man in Mexico might have the Italian name, Graziano. Much thought was needed to make fiction believable. Basically, 'fantasy' had boundaries and rules, in order to be a good read. Readers were a critical lot, and many had eagle eyes for errors and continuity. Substance and accuracy was paramount.

The man sitting next to me struck up a casual conversation, one that became compelling. He was a 'local' but preferred to chat with out-of-towners. He worked on the adjacent wharf and was the manager and the owner of a local charter fishing service—a large one. He had his captain's license but he relied on others to take people out fishing for 'blues' or flounder. The odd thing was he did not reek of fish. Like 'gentlemen farmers,' he was a 'gentleman fisherman' who owned the business but was high enough in management and stature to avoid the blood and guts of the hands-on business. He had a fleet of specialty charter boats, each one of substantial monetary value.

"Where ya from?" he asked, with a Boston accent. "Round here?"

"I grew up here in the North End but live in Western Massachusetts in the woods, so to speak. You?" I asked.

"Native Bostonian," he said. "Grew up in Southie."

"What's your name?" I asked cordially. He replied, "Smitty. Yours?"

"I'm John," I replied. "Pleasure to meet ya."

"What'da ya do?" he asked, spreading his hands apart in an Italian gesture. He shrugged his shoulders. "For work, I mean."

"Write," I replied. "I'm a writer . . . of novels."

"Really," he said, surprised. "You famous?"

"Do I look famous?" I answered, with a grin. "If I was . . . would I not be buying everyone around us a beer?" I was joking.

He seemed to chuckle. "Guess you'd be surrounded by fans. What'd ya write?"

"I've written some stories but you may not have heard of them. I'm still waiting to be discovered."

"Me too," he added with a smile. "I want to retire," he offered. "I can't. Everyone needs two jobs today just to get by. I'm 61 and they tell me I'll have to wait till I'm 67 to get some two-grand a month. Some retirement. Politicians have been pickin' away at Social Security. Our kids will have nothing."

"Know the feeling," I said. "I have a young kid and one on the way. College costs hundreds of thousands today. I *need* a book to become a *movie*."

"Movie? Hell, make an X-rated flick or two with your stories. You'll be rich in no time."

I laughed and almost felt beer come out of my nose. I sipped again from the glass and chuckled. The man was right. I was in the wrong business.

A film of one of my movies would not match the marketability of a bawdy flick that had worldwide distribution.

"What brings you to Boston if you live in the woods?"

"I'm buying my old boyhood home in the North End . . . this weekend. Deal's in progress."

"Congrats," he said, shaking my hand. The I-talian section is fun."

I had noticed that many people pronounced the word I-talian, not It-talian. I once had a friend that grew up in Wisconsin. It was I-talian to him as well. I never understood why.

"You from Wisconsin?" I asked him. He looked at me strange.

"Nah . . . always been from Southie. Why?"

I told him of my friend from the 'Cheese State' and that his pronunciation of words was similar. He was quick to say that he had a Boston accent, born and bred here.

We chatted about the Red Sox and he informed me that he had worked at Fenway Park as a kid, hawking peanuts and soda. We spent an hour on the history of the 1912 park and the players that made the city famous. He was a Doerr, Pesky and Dom DiMaggio fan. I mentioned Ted Williams and Yaz. The more we chatted, the more similar we were in thought.

After some appetizers to hold us over and dilute the beer, I excused myself and paid the tab. I picked up his tab as well. He was grateful of my kindness and wished me luck with my writing, as well as a Happy Christmas. I did the same. "Happy fishing and safe harbor in the new year."

"Maybe see you again," he offered. "I'm here most nights. I'll take you out in the boat sometime. Then we'll eat what we catch. Deal?" We exchanged business cards but his didn't say much on it—only his name and number.

I responded, "Deal, Smitty." We shook hands and I patted him on the back.

As I was leaving, a waitress crossed in front of me, by accident I thought.

"Excuse me," I apologized.

"No problem," she said with a smile. "My fault."

"Do you know who the man was that you were talking to?" she asked, with her hand aside her mouth. I shook my head, no.

"That's Smitty . . . Gordon Smithfield of Boston restaurant fame. He owns the seafood restaurants on Atlantic Avenue, Tremont Street and another one at the Needham Mall. He probably told you 'he was in the fishing business, right?'"

"Why, yes."

He likes people and dresses down to meet people and chat. He is one of the most successful businessmen in the area. He just likes to chat and get to know the public.

"He said he was from Southie," I offered.

"Yah . . . Southie. He's from Southie all right . . . south of Boston, as in *the Cape*, that's Cape Cod! He has a mansion near Hyannis and a condo in the Customs House Clock Tower over there," she said, pointing out the window.

"Really?"

"Yes . . . really!"

"Did you get his card?" she asked.

"Yes," I responded.

"That's his cover . . . the charter boat business. If he has your card, you'll hear from him. I guarantee."

"Why?"

"Because he likes to help people who have passion in their daily life and work. He has been known to help financially, especially people in need."

"Thanks for the tip," I said, handing her a five-dollar bill, just for the holidays. I looked back at the man at the bar and saw that he was still alone. I had the feeling that she could be on to something and that I would be hearing from him. My conversation never addressed money in any way, but I had told him of my desire to make a movie of one of my novels. He had my business card.

Upstairs, in the plush room I stared out the window at the harbor. It looked cold and the boats were few. Susan had awakened from my entry and wanted to know where I'd been. She was worried.

"I was havin' a beer with a local and we got carried away. Nice guy from Southie."

"Come to bed, Honey. Let's get some sleep. I have shopping at Faneuil Hall in the morning. Remember?"

"Yes," I responded, half listening. "Ever heard of Smitty's Restaurants?"

"Can't say that I have," she added, wiping her eyes of sleep. "Why?"

"Ah . . . someone mentioned it was the place for seafood. We'll have to try one over the holidays. There's one by the wharves. Over by Pier 4 on Northern Avenue, I think.

"Sounds good."

In a matter of minutes we were asleep. Sunday morning would come fast. I wanted to show my family the church from my youth and then visit the Faneuil Hall and Quincy Market venues. We still had to shop, and then head home to Western Massachusetts. Snow was predicted for the late afternoon and I wanted to get on the road before it was a major hazard on the Massachusetts Turnpike.

Chapter 19

The beauty of the Faneuil Hall history was impressive in its own right. I wanted Grazie to appreciate its role in the Revolution. Susan was shopping in a lady's dress and handbag shop and my son and I sat on a bench in the morning sun. It was only 32° F and the sun was warming. We had little interest in the store in which Susan would spend one-half hour. She was destined to spend some money for sure. There were ongoing Christmas specials, as evidenced by the large red and white signs in the windows touting 40% off. I knew that on December 26th, the signs would read 60% off and my wife was oblivious to that. She was on a mission to buy. Who could deny her that?

When Susan was done, we ventured through the Food Court at Quincy Market. Grazie spotted a stuffed animal shop nearby and wanted Wally the Green Monster, the Red Sox icon. I bought him a small one for $11.00. As he looked at the other Webkinz and TY Beanies, I picked up a map of the marketplace stores that surrounded the Hall. I had remembered some of the history of the famed building. It was one of the oldest. The brochure told me much more that I found fascinating.

In 1742, Faneuil was fabricated as a meeting hall and marketplace. Known as the 'Cradle of Liberty,' the original building was constructed by John Smibert from 1740-1742. The style was Georgian and fashioned after an English country market. A man by the name of Peter 'Fanuel' funded the project, hence his name on the Hall. His name had changed in spelling and was even pronounced differently. Eventually, it became Faneuil. The 'market' included sheep from New Hampshire that were housed in pens.

The original Faneuil Hall burned in 1761. By 1762, Charles Bulfinch was responsible for expanding it. Samuel Adams had preached there advocating a separation from England.

From 1898 to 1899, the building was basically rebuilt/renovated, but the Main Hall where patriots spoke, remained as original as possible.

Once outside, Grazie noted the weathervane on top of the building. It was placed there in 1742. It remains to this day, a copper and gold leaf 'grasshopper.' It originally stood atop a building at William and Mary College in Williamsburg, Virginia. Weighing 38 lbs. and 52" long, it is a little known piece of art in history. True Bostonians know of it, but visitors ponder it daily. The glass eyes of the grasshopper were thought by many to be fabricated from old doorknobs. Shem Drowne, the artisan who fabricated the weathervane, is buried in Copp's Hill Burial Ground as were others of note, namely the Mather family of local ministers and a shipyard owner of prominence, Edmund Hartt.

I pointed out the history of the grasshopper weathervane to my son. He shook his head and said, "Dad, why is it not a cow or fish. That would be normal."

I laughed and retorted, "We'll find out more of its history when we get home."

Sometimes kids have the right perspective. It was Boston and a fish from the nearby wharves, or a cow for New England would have been a better choice than a bug in the grass.

Back inside the marketplace rotunda, we saw a sign for meeting Santa. He was sitting in a bright red chair fit for a king. The set was basically the North Pole décor with a few people in line. We lucked out since Graziano begged us to meet Santa. The chair, in which the jolly man sat, was on risers with elves and Mrs. Claus at his side. Lighted trees surrounded the ornate felt wing chair in which he sat. The sign said,

Photos with Santa—$5.00

We managed to get in line and watched as other children sat on his lap to tell him his or her wishes for Christmas. In twenty minutes or less, it was our turn and Grazie walked up unafraid of the large man in the red suit.

The quintessential Santa typified Old St. Nick. He was big in stature and jovial, red-cheeked and all. He was a perfect model for a storybook, his beard long and white and natural. He didn't need pillows under the suit. Obviously, he was well fed and exuded the aura of the man from the North Pole. Mrs. Claus wore tiny glasses like Santa and peered over them, often handing out cookies to impatient children in line. She winked at the parents. Between visitors, Santa would place his elbows on his knees and clasp his fingers. Leaning forward, he appeared less intimidating to the next child that approached.

Santa laughed when Grazie sat on his lap. Grazie had whispered something special in his ear. Santa seemed to listen carefully and he appeared in no hurry to let our son go. He smiled for the photo and the woman attendant, dressed like a green pixie, handed us the Polaroid picture, which developed in a very short time. We elected the Polaroid over the optional digital 8" X 10" matted photo that cost a heck of a lot more.

Mrs. Claus commented.

"He doesn't usually spend that much time with each child. They must be having a special conversation."

I agreed and said that I was sorry for the delay. There were other children waiting.

"It doesn't matter," she offered, "Santa has the option to chat a while and he's the boss."

When Grazie returned to his mother and father I asked him what he and Santa had talked about for so long.

"I can't say, Daddy. It's a secret. I did tell him he would have to come in the door of our new home."

"Why?" I asked, playing dumb. Grazie was quick to tell me that he saw no fireplace or chimney in the new condo.

"I had to tell him not to look for the chimney since there *wasn't* one. I told him I was worried."

"What'd he say to you?" I asked, inquisitively, focusing on the chimney comment.

"He told me that he would find a way in. He mentioned that I should get a 'Christmas Key'—a key to the house." That made my life easier, I thought.

"Okay. Did you tell him what you wanted for Christmas?" I asked.

"Sure," he voiced, with assertiveness. "That's the part I can't tell you, Dad."

"I'm glad that you got to see him. Christmas is just around the corner. You probably want to write him a letter anyway when we get home," I added. "We need to remind him of what you want." Susan winked at me and nodded.

I assured Graziano that we'd get *that key* and make sure that it hung where Santa could see it. I didn't share much more than that and soon the conversation changed to the festivities nearby. Our son was enthralled with the noise and lights that flashed in the historic rotunda. It was the perfect ending to a great weekend.

* * *

The trip to home was uneventful. The Massachusetts Turnpike was free flowing and traffic was light. By the time we reached our little town of Washington, the family was relaxed and comfortable. There was 'something' to returning to the woods.

Toward that end, we relaxed by the fire and talked about our weekend, the world-wind tour of the North End. Graziano was happy to be home. He enjoyed Boston but he was accustomed to his own room and bed. He added Wally the Green Monster to his animal collection on the shelf and then lay down with his iPod. Grazie loved music and he quickly fell asleep.

Chapter 20

Our return to the town of Washington meant that much had to be accomplished prior to Christmas. We had less than two weeks to get organized and there were local festivities, which Graziano was involved in, at school and after school.

There was a Christmas play, which was to be performed one week before Christmas vacation. Grazie was a shepherd in the play and rehearsals were almost every day after school. The production involved the play, a choral concert and holiday activities in his classroom as well.

One of the after school activities was an annual skating party on the forthcoming Friday night. The local playing field had been cleared by town vehicles, flooded by the volunteer fire department and kept free of snow squalls so that there would be a smooth surface for the 6 P.M. to 9 P.M. event.

Mr. Mitchell, from the local gas station and towing service, always offered his large bob-house as a warming hut for the kids. He had built the large structure himself, and it was mounted on skids of wood for easy towing to the center of local ponds and lakes, where he often ice fished. Each year, during the skating party, he would use the tow truck to deliver it to the edge of the local rink. The children would take a break from skating to warm up in the structure, complete with Styrofoam cups of hot chocolate and miniature marshmallows to warm their hands. It was large enough to hold ten kids at a time and they rotated in and out of the miniature home like busy ants on a summer day. The origin of the name, bob-house is attributed to the little sheds that were not removed before the ice thawed in spring. If they were left out to long, the lakes melted in April and the shed, being made of wood, would float or 'bob.'

Inside the bob-house was a small caboose stove from an old train car and a crooked stovepipe to vent the smoke. He burned small pieces of oak to heat the room. The bob-house was complete with a kitchenette where the moms would make hot cocoa and serve cookies. On the walls of the bob-house were photos of fishing derbies past, and large lake trout and bass that had been caught each year. Some were acclaimed trophy winners (record fish) from nearby lakes in Massachusetts. Fold down beds were used in winter when Mr. Mitchell and his sons slept out in the bob-house on weekend trips. All that was missing from this hut was a TV, which no one needed anyway. There were boxes for fishing equipment, which served the dual purpose of seating—stuffed pillows were placed on top of the piano-hinged covers. The kids could sit and warm themselves before returning to the rink.

There was a temporary electrical line for lighting the skating rink in the evening and floods were illuminated brightly for the annual event. The supplemental lighting was provided by a local contractor who happened to own numerous tripods of halogen lights, normally used for building homes, before the interior lighting was installed.

Because not every child could fit in the 'universal' bob-house, one parent always brought a 55-gallon drum with air holes drilled at its base, some four inches from the bottom, for ventilation. The drum was used as a campfire of sorts with stacks of wood at the ready. The fire burned bright into the night and children would surround it to warm themselves. One carpenter from the area had created benches and a picnic table for the kids to rest and watch the roaring fire.

The town would go through a half cord of wood just that one night in order to keep the barrel hot and ready. The steel drum radiated heat in all directions, some 360°. Parents hid nips of alcohol in their parkas and often mixed the whiskey or rum with coke or ginger ale. They chatted with each another and caught up on holiday conversations and wintertime tales keeping themselves amused while the kids skated themselves silly, eventually wearing them out.

On the back of Mr. Mitchell's flatbed was a small Honda generator. A nearby tree was ornately decorated with Christmas lights of many colors. The blue spruce was near the makeshift ice rink and the little gas-powered generator provided lighting for the tree, and the illumination of the rink.

Neighbors always looked forward to the event and it culminated in a series of community activities that included at potluck supper at the local Grange. That was usually on a different evening, but it always preceded Christmas.

Although we participated in the local festivities in our town, we were looking forward to the new condo experience centered on Christmas day. This year, Christmas was on a weekend so we planned on being in the North End by the Friday morning preceding the holiday at the very latest. The extended weekend would be spent in Boston. Elena was to mail us the key in the next week. She planned on being away part of the holiday weekend.

*   *   *

Both Susan and I were not sure what Grazie had told Santa when he sat on his lap in the rotunda of Quincy Market. We asked him to write a letter to Santa and remind St. Nick of what he had requested for Christmas.

The local post office in our little town of Washington remains a simple, small white building from the 1700s. It resembles a little depot similar to a train station. The style is akin to the old 1890s clapboard depots; those that were used for the Boston and Albany, Boston and Maine or New York Central RR lines. The B&M stations were two-toned paint in color and unique and usually possessed ornate roofline architecture that was gingerbread in nature or scrolled wood embellishments. This little building for the U.S. Mail has a similar type roof and overhang and resembles depots that had platforms and winged roof covers that protected the baggage and trunks from inclement weather. The porch has a railing and a deacon's bench for the locals to sit and cogitate or peruse their mail. Inside, the mailbox facing plates are brass doors with combination locks. They are old, but functional. A small window area exists for purchasing stamps, and is decorated by a metal gate that seems both protective and artistic in nature. In the old days, bank tellers had a similar protective facing. The entire lobby of the post office is quaint and warm in nature.

A picket fence surrounds the property and yews of varying sizes spread underneath the windows. Crosshatched windowpanes exude a traditional 'Norman Rockwell setting' in winter. Snow accumulation often builds up in the corners of windows like crescent moon ice crystals seen in a Christmas card of old.

Painted white, like most New England town buildings, the post office has a postal clerk who places a mailbox in the lobby for 'Letters to Santa' each December. Children hand-write letters to him and address the envelopes to *Santa, North Pole*. A return address is required for him to write back to you. No stamp is needed—the letter is free!

A week before Christmas, children who had written to him received a stocking in their mailbox. The stockings usually have a coloring book, crayons, candy canes and plastic toys related to Christmas. The letter the child submits in the 'special mailbox' is returned to the parents of the child. The secret list to Santa no longer remains a secret. Mom and Dad know. Local merchants work in concert with the postal office staff by providing the stocking stuffers, gratis. It's a true community effort and keeps the spirit going each year.

"What did you ask for?" I baited Graziano, gingerly.

"I can't say," replied my son, protectively. "If I told you, I'd never get anything. It's a secret."

"Oh," I responded, "maybe I should write to Santa myself."

"What would you ask him for?" he chided me.

"I can't say. Remember the rule?"

"I'll bet it's a new car or SUV," he tried, again.

"Only Santa and I would know," I insisted.

The previous year and just before last Christmas, our seven-year-old 'Golden' had died of a kidney ailment. Grazie had never gotten over the loss and this year I was concerned that he would be depressed. He had a Christmas ornament and the dog's picture framed in it and he planned to hang it on this year's tree. Susan had kept other pictures of the pet as well. I dreaded the thought of Grazie's much anticipated sadness over the holidays. The previous year's festivities were almost ruined by the loss of his best friend and family member. Rusty was a great animal—gentle, smart and always exuded unconditional love. The dog would roam the backyard, which was extensive. He would follow us to the stream and waterfall where Grazie and I had recently cooked hotdogs over an open fire. Rusty never wandered away and his sad demise at a young age was devastating to everyone in the family.

Two days after Graziano had placed his letter to Santa in the red mailbox, the post office returned the letter to Susan and me in an official USPS opaque envelope. While Grazie was at school we read his note to Santa. The one and only 'important' item on the list was 'a puppy.' We had thought that he wouldn't desire replacing Rusty this soon but it was clear when we read the letter, that we were mistaken. I was hoping for other things to appear on the list, but there were few requests that matched the desire of a dog. With it two weeks before Christmas, and the realization that we would be away in Boston for the holidays, I was stymied as to how I could make his Christmas wishes a reality.

It wouldn't be easy.

Chapter 21

In recent years, I had become a 'homebody.' I had no desire for nightlife, the bar scene or acquaintances that had not outgrown the party atmosphere. My life revolved around my family, much as it does today. My energy transposed into teaching my son about life in general and answering his questions on ubiquitous subject matter that seemed to vary daily. The *soup de jour* was his topic of the day at school perhaps and I have never been at a loss for answers to his questions; some were actually based on tried and true facts, the others on personal experience.

It was much more rewarding than hangin' out with old friends. Oddly enough, I had many old contacts with friends from college. They often wrote to me after reading some alumni newsletter that hyped my writing. That was rewarding and cathartic. I lived for memories, it seemed. *Why else would I want the condo in the North End?*

Aging, good or bad, made me more introspective and mortally conscious, or even philosophical. Age brought wisdom and the quiet times of reflection. I decided that if religion played no roll in someone's life, *why exactly were we here to begin with?* If it was for the betterment of man and the earth, we had *failed* to date. The irony of it all was and is, that most wars are and were started over religion and territories. Man only comes together one day a year to be kinder, that day is Christmas. I guess I've had much time to reflect over the years and *writing* has become my medium to 'voice' my thoughts and opinions. I have always said that 'if one has an opinion and doesn't share it publicly, one has no opinion at all.'

I love the house that I live in, in Washington for many reasons. There is serenity in the woods of New England and in this case, the Berkshires.

Although it's been a hike to Beckett or Pittsfield for major household staples and serious shopping, there is something to be said for the darkness at night in our yard, summer or winter. I have grown accustomed to seeing stars on a clear night. Lying on a blanket in the backyard at midnight and staring straight up on a cool, fall night is wondrous and refreshing—awe-inspiring and never boring, yet ever changing like the phases of the moon. Life changes but the moon has witnessed all of it and has remained constant from millennia to millennia.

Christmas has made life purposeful and has played a significant roll throughout my life's existence it seems. Easter reinforces the waning 'good will' for a while longer. A movie that helped me refocus and impacted my philosophy was *King of Kings* in 1961. Jeffrey Hunter was the greatest actor to portray Christ. His eyes and facial structure were the epitome of what one thinks of the eyes of the Lord. Sadly, he died at 42 years-of-age, from complications of a stroke and a fall in 1969. His image and blue eyes remain to this day—ever piercing and convincing that Christ must have been handsome and patient. Although Hunter starred in thirty-two films, the one that impacted me was *that one* film.

Today, the world revolves too fast—we all need to slow down a bit and show some empathy and love. Christmas is love!

The woods and Mother Nature in general have inspired me to write more descriptively in my novels. The simplest things in life are—truly free. They are the wonders of the natural world and they're available without monetary cost.

Winter had brought its challenges. Being so far out from our neighboring towns or cities in Western Massachusetts often required shoveling oneself out just to go *anywhere*—to the post office or local convenience store for bread or milk.

Our driveway is a quarter-mile long requiring a simple Fisher plow on a truck to keep things clear. The Chevy truck accomplishes the task, except when it is not running on all six. It's an older model that I had bought locally from a neighbor for 'a grand.' It even lacks four-wheel drive but pushes that plow just the same. It's a standard three-speed and we use it for dump runs, spreading loam in the spring or merely for grocery runs, locally. The truck remains boring gray and often requires simple tune-ups—plugs, points, rotor and a cap.

Much of what is needed mechanically, for the truck to run, I can achieve myself—oil changes and the like. Simple stuff. Graziano has taken an interest in those needed upgrades to the 'gray goose.' I often let him help with repairs. More serious repairs require the local garage, an inexpensive alternative for handling the major issues. I avoid the occasional brakes, transmission and muffler repairs which the locals are pleased to fix at a whim. It keeps the money in the town and not at the specialty muffler shop in Pittsfield.

With the impending trip to Boston forthcoming, I needed to make sure that the home in Washington was accessible. The truck, an Ariens snow blower, and a couple of shovels made life much easier for us to clear the snow. Even the Ariens engine had a new short block and an orange-colored repaint. It was approaching 20 years in age and had a 32" carriage—hard to find these days. Grazie kept the front steps and sidewalk clear while I focused on access to and from the house by drive, and the long serpentine paths to the shed and garage area.

This one particular day, I had finished clearing all that had accumulated from the recent snowfall. I entered the mudroom and hung my plaid jacket and cap on separate hooks. The gloves were placed on a small radiator to dry and my boots sat out on the stoop. I looked something like a Norman Rockwell painting all by myself. Long underwear was needed due to the chill and my face was red from the wind swept snow that sometimes abraded my cheeks. I felt invigorated at any rate and merely wanted to relax in my recliner in the den.

Susan had made ginger snaps for Grazie and hot chocolate for both of us. After a brief time changing in the entryway, I smelled the enticing aroma of baked cookies, which permeated the nearby rooms and hall. Barefoot and cold, I meandered to the kitchen.

"Ya done, Hon?" she asked.

I nodded, yes. My cheeks remained flushed and my hands were cold.

"Have a rest and try this new cocoa. It's not Swiss Miss but a high-end brand of San Francisco chocolate that a cookbook had recommended." Grazie sat by me as we sipped the hot delight. Susan was preparing dinner, a stew or thick soup of beef stock and vegetables. The cookie smell prevailed. Life couldn't be better.

"I'm gonna move out to the den," I said, carrying the large mug with a Christmas logo on it. Susan busied herself and Grazie retreated to his room with the small TV and some DVD movies that he especially liked to watch over and over again. Harry Potter and all the iterations of the series could occupy him for hours. He had read many of the Harry Potter books as well, a seemingly unusual task for an eight-year-old. He had excelled at reading early on often accomplishing and absorbing teenage literary works with ease.

*   *   *

The fresh air and chill, along with the recliner, was no match for my fatigue following the hour-and-a-half process of eliminating the recent white powder that had left us with eight inches from the recent storm. Flurries were evident even as I felt the chair envelop me like a hotdog roll. It was the brown leather one once again and comfortable. In front of me was an aquarium, only 10 gallons, but dimly illuminated from above and sparkling clean. It had a rocky ledge and fake plant background while the small pump aerated the water with a gentle bubbling sound.

The fish in the serene tank were nothing special. As a matter of fact, they were pretty common species. There were swordtails, neon tetras, guppies, mollies, a catfish and one angel. The only belligerent meanie in the tank was the angel, which we named, 'Killer.' Its job was to harass the others into oblivion it seemed. It had already taken one tail off a guppy, one that was evidently too slow to escape. The milfoil plant life, acquired from a local pond, gave ample protection and camouflage for the fish that were chased by Killer. Even the fertile guppies procreated every 30 days or so to keep new fry in the tank. They hid in the weeds until they were larger in size and could fend for themselves.

To the right of the fish tank were a bookcase and a stereo system with many CDs stacked alphabetically. Today, my mood was for an *IL Divo* or the *Gord's Gold* CD, a greatest hits album by Gordon Lightfoot. I rose from the chair and selected the 'random' button on the CD changer. I extended the earphone cord long enough to reach the chair and grabbed the remote which had slid down into the side of the recliner. It was there with a few old gum wrappers and the occasional piece of popcorn or M&M.

The first song that played was *Mama* by *Il Divo* and then *Song for a Winter's Night* from the *Gold* album played afterward. Lightfoot is a master at words and melodies. This *Winter's Night* song he claims to have conceived on a rainy day in Cleveland, Ohio. It wasn't even winter when he wrote it, but you find yourself transposed into a snowbound cabin in the Maine woods with nothing more that an oil lamp or nearby candle. The song paints the picture of snow, cold, and frosted windows as a man sits at a table pining for his lover.

The late afternoon lack of sun darkened the wood paneling in the den and the serenity of the fish tank and music facilitated everything I needed to relax. My mind was in neutral and I had no cares in the world. I felt sorry for those humans that could not, or had not the ability to unwind. Day jobs can be hard on the human body and mind, and a nine-to-five routine that my dad once knew must have been a grind. He worked six days a week and had little time to enjoy his family or the amenities, which I took for granted as a child. I was humbled by the thought that life had been pretty good to me thus far. I 'had it all' so to speak, and was even destined by fate to acquire my boyhood home again.

In less than five minutes of relaxation I was asleep and the headphones were still set at 6 out of 10 in volume. Apparently, Susan had come into the darkened room, removed my headset and kissed the top of my head (she later acknowledged). She claimed that I hadn't budged.

Life could be no better than that and the Christmas holidays were right around the corner. A CD of Italian phrases 'for everyday use' sat nearby. Later that week I would try to relearn, or venture to remember, the incredible romantic language of my forefathers. Over the Christmas holidays, I wanted to be able to chat a bit with the locals in the North End. Seemingly impossible, due to time constraints, I still would make a valiant effort to achieve that quest of relearning Italian.

Chapter 22

Having waken from my snooze, I noticed the hand-crocheted blanket that covered me during my brief departure from reality. I felt rested and knew that Susan or Grazie had taken the time to cover me during my slumber. Thoughtfulness always ran in their minds and I loved them for caring, whether it was for a family member or for a friend. Graziano was beginning to emerge as an independent person and I think, thus far, we had done a nice job of teaching him Emily Post's manners and compassion for both man and beast. He loved animals like the rest of us and would probably make a great veterinarian someday. He leaned that way, even at an early age, surpassing the 'fireman phase.' Once his aspirations were beyond the avocation of being a fireman, I suspect he would lean more toward wildlife preservation or animal doctoring.

My eyes were cloudy having inadvertently left my contact lenses in them while I slept. It always happens when, in haste, I think that I am just going to rest a while and end up sleeping a couple of hours. I blinked repeatedly and stared at the ceiling until they seemed to clear. Proteins in eye fluids always did it. Eventually, normal tearing would clear the obvious discomfort and cloudiness.

Rarely do I remember my dreams, but this particular rest startled me and I awoke to various memories and nostalgia. The dream had been in color, a rarity for me since most dreams I *do* remember are black and white images, fabricated by a confused brain, with people and places that seem real but are unknown persons to me. When I was younger, all dreams appeared that way—no one I knew was in them; it was a cadre of fictitious faces, bodies and places I had never known or been to. As I aged and turned forty, I found myself dreaming *in color* with characters and towns in those scenarios, comprised of actual places and people that I remembered in my life. Some were from my youth and that scared me a bit. Why the transition from black and white to color, and why were the characters in my subconscious now people who currently are, or were, from my life's experiences?

The fish tank continued to bubble as I watched the ceiling fan, preset in reverse motion, so the fan blades guided the warm air (of the wood stove) down from the ceiling, back to floor level. When heat rises, one must find a way to recapture it on the coldest days, especially with cathedral ceilings.

It was still snowing when I sat up and pondered the recent 'mental film' from the past.

In the dream, I clearly remembered seeing my childhood friends, Aldo and Dominick. We were playing on the swings in a nearby park. We were inseparable and each day in summer we checked with each other to see what we were going to do that particular day. We 'Three Musketeers' always had ideas or simple agendas while our parents worked. We were sure to be home by 5 P.M. for dinner, but during the daytime hours, we might migrate a mile or so in any direction. We would fish off a wharf on Commercial or New Atlantic Avenues. We might ride bikes to Faneuil Hall or seek out an abandoned building for a game of 'hide and seek.' The only thing that really frightened us was not the other person in the game, but the occasional rat that appeared in the shadows. They were common by the water, ironically seeking food in daylight when they normally were nocturnal predators. They are supposed to come alive at night, not during the day. Often, construction jobs or renovated building activities by contractors scared them up from their slumber.

We 'boys' were a *clique* of sorts, and few girls penetrated 'this trio's' agenda. By the time I was a teenager, I noticed other things besides my male cohorts. One homegrown beauty was a girl named Nancy DiGiulio. She was a local and in our school class. She grew up like most girls do, in that there was an awkward period—age eleven to thirteen for females. She blossomed into a stunning young woman with brunette hair, often worn long or tied back in a ponytail. She somehow appeared in this dream with Aldo and Dom. I remember her wanting to fit in, to be a part of the infamous trio, but we shunned her in arrogance. As a teen however, the brain functioned differently. All three of us found her attractive and the competition began as to who was going to take her to the movies. We used to bet nickels and dimes on that. Nancy was too smart and self-poised to put up with our shenanigans. She knew that we treated her poorly or teased her during her younger years when she appeared all teeth, or too thin to compete with us in games or sports.

Where we went afoul, were the days that eventually passed. Her appearance changed into a maturing young lady, somewhere after her Confirmation at St. Leonard's. It was obvious that she would be a beauty like her mother, Christina. There was no looking back at us for her, after we dissed her all those years. A boy from another school in Boston picked up on her natural beauty and softness and managed to date her at sixteen. He was Randall Clay and he came from money in Newton. She outclassed us and we knew it. Why she appeared in this dream was beyond me. I guess 'we three' always pined for her having realized we had lost her as a friend or potential girlfriend.

In the later years, I read of her doing very well in college in Northampton. She was a 'Smith girl' and landed a job in New York City. From time to time, I would read of her success in business and impending marriage to a doctor who specialized in neurosurgery.

Nancy DiGiulio was a stunner and I assume that she raised a family. My hope was that one day we would reconnect, perhaps in the North End and revisit our youth. After all, I had found Aldo's son by chance. Fate, being what it is, shed little doubt that, down the line many of us from the North End would eventually find one another at a class reunion or some serendipitous get together.

I managed to sit up in the chair just as Susan appeared with a cup of coffee. Darkness had now set in but the backyard floodlight illuminated the snow that fell on this windless night. The huge flakes seem to resist falling as she and I watched the show from a sliding glass door. They seemed to stay aloft avoiding their demise in a massive pile of their siblings, billions of them suspended in animation before landing.

"Did you have a nice rest?" she asked, followed by a peck on the cheek. She was lovely even in the darkened room.

"For sure. Why didn't you wake me?"

"I didn't want to disturb the 'roar of the snore,'" she commented, in jest. "You looked so comfortable in that chair, mouth open and relaxed to the point of exasperation," she offered. I didn't smile, for the image of a 'virtual' death mask was not favorable.

"Did you at least close my mouth and cross my arms on my chest?" I asked, expecting a morbid joke.

"No," she replied, smiling, "I recorded the sounds on a digital recorder for posterity. I think a visit to the doctor is finally due, My Love. You may have sleep apnea."

"Nah."

"Well—you surely were holding a breath or two. Doesn't that indicate that you might have an issue?"

"Nah," I answered, in denial.

She wouldn't let up. "Perhaps *that* can be your New Year's resolution—to see someone about *that* problem."

"Okay. I can do that," I said, to appease her.

"Fine. I need to see if Grazie 'crashed' as well. He wanted to do what his father was doing. Rest with music. I'll go check his room."

"Like father, like son," I responded, chuckling.

"For sure," she agreed. "I'll be right back."

Graziano had in fact slumbered off as well, complete with his glasses still on. The difference was that he didn't snore and I did. He would end up sleeping the whole night in his clothes much akin to what I did as a child. The clearing of snow had taken its toll on both of us and Susan was the only one who survived the slumber party. She had baked and cooked and managed to clean the kitchen all in one. Grazie and I were lucky men.

It was now *her* time to rest. She decided to read a book. That lasted about two pages and she was out. I managed to watch some sports show on TV for a couple of hours and often switched to a weather-related channel to stay abreast of the newest updates. More was coming!

I would be back out in the driveway the very next day. There was no mercy this particular winter. 'Mother Nature' or the 'Man Above' was destined to keep the white fluff around for a white Christmas, either here or in Boston.

*　　*　　*

The beauty of residing in the woods, especially in a spacious older home, meant there were ample places to store stuff—stuff that we collected all our lives and brought back into the house after a yard sale that failed. In the summer, especially around July 4th, we often tried to sell stuff that we didn't want or need. It's amazing what one family can collect—stuff that's not needed. For some odd reason, we think that most collections of tools, toys, figurines, pottery and holiday decorations increase in value with age. They don't for the most part, merely becoming 'dust collectors.'

The most valuable items that I had hoarded as a child were no different than items in other homes with kids. I had baseball cards, American Flyer and Lionel train sets and knickknacks that my mother had kept in a china cabinet. When I grew older, my dad had packed most of that stuff away. The boxes shifted from attics to cellars, closets to any available space under the beds. I repeat, they were 'dust collectors' and that's all.

Today's junk has no comparison in value to the items my dad had. The reason why the old stuff was valuable today is because my father *tossed it out* en masse when I grew older and left home for college. If it was *gone*, it instantly became *valuable*, because I no longer owned it!

Grazie's toys and my tools have no real value and neither do the old TVs that are now being replaced with paper-thin plasma screens of high definition. All our appliances that we kept for 'yard sale' in the past, never sold. They ended up back in the shed, cellar or attic. People don't buy kids clothes either so they are stored in plastic tubs until we can get to Goodwill in Pittsfield.

The baseball cards and the train sets of my youth were classics by today's standards. Some sets of cards, dating back to the 1940s-1950s, were Bowman and Topps brands and are now worth tens of thousands of dollars. The train sets, which were fabricated of heavy metal engines and cars, on a three-railed alternating current track, were reliable for decades and not made of plastic like today's HO lines. The O-gauge (32mm/1.25inch wide tracks) and O-scale (1:43-48 sized engines/cars) were standard Christmas presents in the 1930s-1960s. My dad tossed all those items out. That was my intended partial inheritance from my father I suppose, but the collections disappeared.

In my collection of old things however was my Uncle John's memorabilia from his days working for (and not on) the railroad. He was my mother's brother-in-law and John looked like George Washington in profile—an amazing resemblance to the first president.

To this day, I have some of the railroad artifacts that he acquired while performing his duties as a signal inspector and later manager for the B&A and NYC railroads. His tour of duty was Utica, NY to Boston, but often from Pittsfield to Springfield, Massachusetts. He lived in the Berkshires as well and was born there.

The essential things to his collection were railroad lithographs of Streamliners, old locks and keys, door pulls from depots, kerosene lanterns from the NYC and B&A railroads and documents, route maps and handwritten conductor's logs from his days on the rail. Most of the papers were emblazoned with the insignias of the companies that he had worked for, for years. Many of those railroad lines have disappeared.

One box had a series of locks for trunks, signal equipment and meters that measured voltage and ohms. There were groups of keys that varied in size and were held together by heavy twine or metal rings. Collectors would kill for some of those items but even though they're of value today, I hold on to them at yard sale time. Foolish me!

I only mention these particulars because I had a mission to perform while Graziano was at school. I found the small box of keys in a larger box of lanterns and wheel 'oilers' and the occasional B&M wrench. I was seeking a novel and unique *brass key* for use at Christmas.

The Christmas Chiave was to be a key that I could clean and polish and adorn with a ribbon for the doorway in the North End. Santa needed to visit and I was on a mission to create an heirloom for my son. In the bowels of our cellar, I sorted through many of Uncle John's keys that were sadly embellished with oil, grime and dust from years of improper storage.

One of the keys that stood out was ornate and quite large. It had an artistic sculptured design to the handle and seemed to go to a baggage trunk or railway wall clock, or lock that secured an electrical panel shut at a signal crossing. My guess was that it was from a man's luggage piece or an old clock. Ticket booth wall clocks, like the famed Ball Clock Company had that kind of key for winding the spring. The end of it was hexed not toothed, but Grazie would probably not know the difference in type.

It would be the perfect piece to hang on a hook by the condo door. A red ribbon and a holly branch might dress it up. Susan was ecstatic that I had found the treasure. She agreed with my choice after seeing the others that were coated in filth.

"What a beauty," she offered, caressing the key that I had chosen from the cadre of unique pieces. "I agree," I exclaimed. "I can't think of a better Christmas key for Santa. Grazie will love it."

"Lem'me polish it up," she added, grasping a bottle of brass cleaner from under the kitchen sink cabinet.

"I imagine that it'll shine beautifully," I exclaimed, watching over her shoulder as the tarnish disappeared with a soft cloth. "A 'Christmas key' should be old," she added. "Grazie will be excited that Santa will be able to visit us on Christmas Eve."

"It brings back memories for me as well," I offered, in reflection. "I loved *mine* and wish my father had saved it and passed it on to the family."

Susan stopped for a moment and was deep in thought. She smiled gently and turned around. "You like St. Anthony, right? Isn't he the one saint they celebrate in 'Little Italy'?"

"Yes . . . where are you going with this?"

"He was the Patron Saint of Lost Articles. You should say a little prayer."

"Don't be silly . . . I'm sure that the key my dad had is long gone and in someone's key collection in Somewhere, USA."

"I suppose you're right. It was just a thought, since you grew up in a staunch Catholic family that was very devout. You said your father was pious, right?"

"Oh, yes—church, novenas, prayer sessions, confessions, catechism, holy days, feasts and no meat on Friday, Honey."

"See? You need to take the issue up with St. Anthony." She was smiling and patted my cheek affectionately. "You don't have to do it in church. Just address him in silence. The *Lord* does wonders," she teased, "through others."

Chapter 23

Susan took the time to shop for presents while Grazie was still in school. She didn't even tell her husband where she was going—*just going shopping*, she claimed. She pulled her SUV into the lot of a small bookstore, one that was known for hard to find volumes and rare editions. It was in Beckett, Massachusetts and not far from the town center and general commercial district. Few people could afford the classics that were stacked up as 'first editions' among other cheaper or popular books that were sold to people who merely wanted the latest Patricia Cornwall, Barbara Delinsky or Patterson and Grisham novels of mystery and intrigue.

The most common question to the owner was often, 'when is Dan Brown's next piece due out?' Mr. Bradford, the elderly owner, had no clue as to when the sequel to *The DaVinci Code* might appear. It was rumored in writer's circles that the working title was, *The Solomon Key*.

"May I help you?" he offered, courteously.

She responded in kind, "Yes, please."

After the short greeting and an exchange of the weather conditions, she asked the owner, known locally as Elias, if he had in his collection, any older books that dealt with historic Boston—something other than the standard tourist travel books for everyday sightseeing.

Her focus was on the American Revolution and the later history of the 1800s-1900s. She was aware from conversations with her husband that the North End and Old State House/ Faneuil Hall areas underwent remarkable periods of growth, including the follow on eras of immigration by many different, ethic peoples.

She was savvy. She knew from the Internet that the North End was not always Italian in nature but a 'melting pot' of many influences and people from England, its Isles, Africa and Europe. Historically, the New World adventurers had trades or expertise that varied: first were the fruit vendors, then the bakers, and later a cadre of fishermen and seamen who utilized Boston Harbor and beyond for their daily catch. Others were tradesmen, stonemasons and bricklayers, carpenters and construction laborers that moved the earth for little pay. They created the wharves, churches, buildings and landmasses that expanded Boston's peninsula inland, making it livable. Marshes and estuaries near the harbor became habitable land. She wanted a book that said all that but one that was old, with historic maps and charts.

Mr. Bradford lowered his reading glasses to the tip of his nose and stroked his chin as if in deep thought.

"Follow me, Ma'am, please," he beckoned with his hand. His leather shoes were unpolished and his pants too short. She followed as he headed to the back of the store and they traversed multiple stacks of books on all subject matters. Some individual signs on the shelves read, HISTORY, SCIENCE, CLASSICS, SPORTS, LITERATURE and MEDICINE.

He was elderly but his mental faculties were still sharp. He was short and balding with suspenders crisscrossed and attached to his pants. There was an obvious limp from an old injury. He dressed in a wool shirt for winter and guided Susan to the last row of books. Straight ahead was a bookcase that contained a series of glass-covered shelves of oak. The furniture was dusty but the books were protected. The glass case and shelves opened upward and the front panels then slid back into the bookcase like a pocket door of old, only horizontal in action. The antique case was beautiful, in and of itself. RARE BOOKS graced the cabinet top glass panel. To Susan, they *smelled* rare as well.

He fondled some older editions on many subjects. They were hardbound and somewhat yellowed in appearance due to age, at least the pages appeared amber-like from a distance. They must have been exposed to sunlight at some point but had in some way escaped the infamous silverfish that consumed books for food.

He stood silent. Susan stood back a bit as he whistled a tune that was unrecognizable to her. He rocked his head back and forth and studied each shelf one at a time . . . almost fixated or catatonic in a trance. He would look closer and then back off studying each shelf of the uniquely carved bookcase.

"Hmm," he mumbled, "it was here the other day."

"What Mr. Bradford? I'm sorry but I missed what you said. What was here?"

"I was just thinking out loud," he said. "I saw a book the other day that's been here forever. It has a lot to do with Old Boston, the Quincy Marketplace and parts of the waterfront. I'm sure that the North End is in there as well . . . old maps of the streets and stuff. It's unique."

"Do you remember the name?" Susan asked. "I can help you look, perhaps," she offered, straining to look beyond his shoulder for a clue—the words, *Boston, North End, Little Italy,* anything close.

Mr. Bradford seemed to be cogitating, often rubbing his forehead back and forth with the first two fingers of his left hand.

"The author was Ponti I think—perhaps Francis Ponti as I recall. The title has something to do with the word, island. Yes, the *Island of North Boston*—it's right here. My eyes are failing me, Ma'am."

"Can't be failing you, Mr. Bradford. You spotted it after all . . . see?"

Bradford handed the volume to Susan with both hands and she studied the leather cover. It seemed in good shape but one would need to be careful when turning the pages, she thought. Bookbindings were often sewn and, if glued, would be dried out over the years—especially with volumes of that age. Susan perused the table of contents and was pleased to see that the North End history covered the Revolutionary War, the immigration of the Irish, Portuguese, Jews and Italians. Of particular interest to her was the changing topography of the land near the harbor, a portion of which was a peninsula that was backfilled to create a direct link to Boston 'Proper.' Many immigrants helped create the changing landscape of the North End, Beacon Hill and the Back Bay.

"Think that will do ya?" asked Bradford, who was waiting patiently for her to decide on the book. "It's quite old."

"How much is it?" she asked, knowing the price could be hefty.

"You a research professor?" he asked her. "People who buy that kind of book usually are in grad school or are a teacher, ya know, a scholar."

"No, Sir. It's for my husband. He grew up in the North End and I'm getting it for him for Christmas. We just bought a second home there and the home was his original boyhood residence. He's a writer and has an extensive library of his own in our den."

Bradford blinked and asked what his name was.

"He's Giovanni Perri, but goes by John. He writes novels."

"Know the name," he retorted. "I've read some of his works . . . talented writer of fiction. You live nearby right?"

"Yes, we live in Washington, just up the road." Susan found the man enchanting.

"Swears a lot, right?"

"Pardon?" she said, somewhat surprised by the comment. She raised one eyebrow.

"In his books!" he offered.

"Oh, I thought you meant he used profanity in front of you."

Bradford laughed. "No Ma'am. I was referring to his writing. I like his style. Says it like it is. I admire one who writes truthfully."

Susan looked relieved. "I thought he might have offended you in person, Mr. Bradford. That's a relief."

"Nah. The man uses the 'F' word where it's needed. We ain't prudes here in this business. I kinda like that."

Bradford managed to smile for the first time.

"Look," he said. "I discount books for authors, good authors. That book would run you $150, normally . . . but for Mr. Perri, I can do you $75. Is that fair? He's an author that I admire."

"More than fair, and nice of you," she responded, nodding.

He laughed. "It's Christmastime and consider that an early gift. Please bring him by someday. I'd like to meet him in person."

"I surely will. He has mentioned you many times but I don't think he's ever met you. You know those writers, they're reclusive," she smiled.

"I'm the one that's reclusive," he volunteered. "Half the time, I'm never open. I can't get around much anymore and my kids have all moved away, far way."

"I'm sorry, Mr. Bradford. We'll have you over some day, if that's okay with you."

"Thanks," he added. "That'd be nice. By the way, what's your name?"

"Susan. I should apologize for not introducing myself earlier. Please call me *Susan*."

"Call me Elias, please. Pleasure to meet you."

Susan settled the bill, wished him a Merry Christmas and gave the old man a holiday hug. She sat in her car for five minutes and perused the volume, which was more information than her husband would ever need. Of particular interest was the Chapter on the immigration of the Italians after the Irish and Jewish settlements in the North End. The Italians came over in droves eventually boasting some 44,000 persons in the one square-mile area.

What were impressive in the volume were the chapters on each specific area from which the migrations occurred. First were the people of Genoa, Campani, Sicily; then the Avellinese, Nepolitanos and people from Abruzzi. Her husband had relatives from both Abruzzi and Calabria. It would be the perfect gift.

*   *   *

While my wife went shopping and Grazie was in school, I got stuck with clearing snow again. It had been one of the worst winters and it wasn't even the holidays yet. We had a couple months of winter to go and there had already been an accumulation of more than 36" to date. It broke a record for the Berkshires for total snowfall before Christmas, at least in our town.

When Susan returned home, I noticed one bag of goodies was from a local bookstore that was known for older editions of the Classics and rare finds. Few people cared about them or could afford them. Some scholars had a hard time finding many of the rarities. I personally had never been in the shop. It was always closed when I passed by. It was often 'seasonal' for store hours. I always wanted to meet the old man that ran it but to date it had been futile. The innocuous and suggestive bag implied that this might be the time to go see him. He was apparently open for the holidays. *Hmm, I thought . . . what had she purchased?*

Quickly and deceptively, Susan headed upstairs, arms loaded with multiple bags; some items straining to stay in the paper bags. She attempted to carry them from the car, in one fell swoop. She had been to more than one store.

I offered to help her with the load and she kindly told me to (basically), 'go away—it's off limits.' Obviously, a potential present for me was in there somewhere and it was a secret, at least for now.

I'd rather be surprised anyway. I behaved like a kid at this time of year.

Chapter 24

Christmas this year was on a Saturday. We intended to head for Boston Thursday night or Friday morning. The beauty of arriving a bit early in the North End would allow us to set up the condo that we were borrowing for the weekend. The finalization of the sale of the property could not transpire until the present owners returned from down south. They desired to be at the closing.

Elena LaFauci, the Realtor, was happy to loan us the key and had in fact mailed it to our home in advance. Susan wanted to make the temporary abode as Christmas-like as possible, mainly for Graziano who would be spending his first Christmas away from our Cape in the Berkshire Mountains.

Although we felt he might be depressed being away from the traditional festivities in our mountain home, he very much looked forward to being in Boston where the action was. He also knew that it would be special for me since I had grown up in that condo decades earlier. Grazie was a considerate child for his age. He had never shown evidence of self-centeredness like some kids his age. He knew that it was a second home in the North End and not a permanent residence that would take him from his friends forever. His flexibility made the process more relaxed and fun for the whole family. As an eight-year-old and soon to be nine, he merely wanted to be assured that Santa would find him in Boston. He had already sat on Santa's lap in Faneuil Hall and expressed his desire for presents.

Both Susan and I were aware that this might be the last year that he would have these dreams or fantasies during the holiday season. Kids, his age or older, would surely exert peer pressure on him concerning Santa and flying reindeer. We wanted him to enjoy this last year of innocence, a season that would have lasting memories for him, and for us.

Christmas was for children we had often said, and *life*, with all its complications, would have impact on his psyche and personal development down the road. Fantasy and the holiday spirit was a relief from the pressures of school, friends who were not always kind, and the final act of growing up in the forthcoming pre-pubescent teenage years. There would be ample time later for the hormonal seesaw and mood swings that accompanied the emergence of a lowered voice, troubles with female friends and girlfriends, and the impending loss of his first 'puppy love.' We were forestalling these future shocking negatives in life by cherishing his single digit, innocent years.

*   *   *

The car, packed to the gills with the boxes needed for Christmas, contained lights for a tree in the North End. There were memorable ornaments from my youth, sprigs of holly from the bush in our yard, presents that were pre-wrapped by my wife and even some basic staples for food. We wanted to leave the condo after Christmas, just the way we found it upon arrival. We were only borrowing the facility, not moving in. We packed our own linens, soap, shampoo and toiletries. Much of the food needs for each meal would be purchased in 'Little Italy.' Susan intended to make it as Italian as possible, sensing that I would appreciate revisiting my youth, at least in my mind. That included patronizing the local food markets, pastry shops, Italian Importing stores and other local shops for wine.

We anticipated that we would eat out much of that weekend, allowing us to partake in local festivities at churches and festivities in honor of the Madonna and Christ child. That way we weren't trapped in the condo cooking all day.

The drive from Washington to Boston was some 120-miles or so, as the crow flies. The Massachusetts Turnpike was a straight shot to the North End, especially after the Big Dig highway project was completed at a cost that broke the budget by millions. The new roads and highway overpasses and tunnels led to the area near the Callahan Tunnel and ran adjacent to the Italian section of Boston. The Big Dig project allowed for pedestrians to cross at surface level from the North End to Faneuil Hall Marketplace without peril. When Route 93 was above ground, the trek was not as easy. The new 'green space' park area above ground connected Boston 'Proper' to the Italian section—a conduit that merged two geographical areas for the first time in over two centuries.

After a two-hour ride on a blue-sky day, Graziano awoke as we negotiated Hanover Street from the Boston side. We made the trip by early afternoon and headed straight to the Prince Street home. It felt odd pulling into the drive beside the condo and my home of old. We parked where the owners name was marked on the brick's of the building. Elena had sent us a temporary residential parking permit.

Graziano was the first one out of the car. He remembered the doorway and ornate woodwork and railings. The snow was still mounted high on the side of the street. Parking on side streets had been discontinued due to the narrow passageway. The late, low afternoon sun in the sky, blocked by buildings, cast a cool shadow over the street—making the alleyways seem even more frigid than they were normally.

We had much to carry upstairs and all three of us grabbed a box or bag, one at a time. The hallway was illuminated with a switch at the bottom of the stairwell. The top landing had a coat rack that we could use after we were done moving the contents of the car into the apartment.

Susan stood silent in the center of the kitchen, and stared. The last few remaining bags were placed on the table by Grazie and me. She seemed overwhelmed by the task. There was much more to bring in from the car, including suitcases for each of us. You'd think we were staying for a month.

She sat down in a kitchen chair for a moment while Graziano checked out the room that would be his own personal space in January. He seemed pleased and Susan seemed exasperated.

I could tell what Susan was thinking—*how she might get the place festive in the short time we were there.* We didn't even have a tree yet and there was nothing in the place to suggest it was the Christmas holidays.

"We have our work cut out for us," she said, quietly and with some trepidation. "Christmas is on Saturday and here we are still unpacked."

"Not to worry," I said, hugging her in consolation. "I'll get the rest of the stuff downstairs and you can sit for a moment. It'll be fine."

She didn't acknowledge my confidence and I thought I saw a tear in one eye. She was used to our home in Washington and this didn't seem like it would come together by Christmas Eve. I had more faith than her. I managed to get a smile out of her after I kissed her cheek. It did seem daunting.

Once we were settled, I could see that Grazie had already opened his belongings and was playing with one or two Christmas decorations—they were a Beanie elf and a snowman. He seemed to adjust well. My old room surrounded him like a glove and he was in the mood.

"Can we get pizza, Dad? I'm starving."

"Once we get settled," I assured him, "we can walk down the street and get you all the pizza you can eat." He smiled at the thought.

My wife was much more pragmatic.

Susan immediately took out a list of things that we needed to accomplish or buy to survive the next few days in a strange place. She was methodical in listing what would be necessities for Christmas itself. There was a 'honeydew' list for each of us to fulfill. We all had assigned chores to make the holiday successful. 'Honey do this, and Honey do that' was the immediate agenda that Susan had in mind. It was aimed more at me than at Graziano and I accepted the assignments willingly to make the transition flow smoothly.

*   *   *

I'd previously let Aldo, Jr. know by phone that we were acquiring the house in which I grew up. He had my cell phone number and had called me once after I'd returned home from the writer's conference. I explained to him that I had located and visited his father's grave, in the deep snow of the Copp's Hill Burial Ground. He appreciated the thoughtfulness and was genuinely thankful. He also knew that we'd be visiting over Christmas and he hoped to meet my family. His family had activities going on as well over the Christmas holidays. It would be tight trying to get together but we promised each other that we would try and hook up. By the time we arrived in Boston that afternoon, his shop was already closed for an extended weekend of religious festivals, prayer services and church events. He had mentioned a 'living Nativity' that they participated in each year. His family stood dressed in period attire and were living actors in the Nativity scene, complete with farm animals, a manger and baby Jesus. The Christ child was a doll since a real child would not have appreciated the cold and snow. Apparently, the Aldo Spinelli family portrayed Mary and Joseph or alternated as the Wise Men and shepherds. The 'living Nativity' was somewhere near Christopher Columbus Park. We would make every attempt to get there and to see them but Susan really wanted to get the house set up.

Our initial plans upon arrival were to get settled and relax, then grab a bite to eat. We still had to find someone who was selling Christmas trees. If there were no trees on the corner of Battery and Commercial Streets like the old days, we might be able to find a selection near Faneuil Hall. I dreaded the thought of bringing one all the way from Quincy Market—an un-welcomed hike with a tree of *any* size.

The plan was to buy the tree on Christmas Eve day, in the early afternoon. We would need a tree stand as well. The local shops would probably have a stand and accessories like lights, balls and tinsel even though there were no hardware stores nearby. Convenience stores that sold snacks and cigarettes had some items in their windows. I had noted that, during the previous trip. Normally, there would be pasta and olive oil bottles in that same store window or biscotti boxes and tomato paste cans. The merchants seemed to know what the public needed, and catered to their every need each holiday.

The North End was self-sufficient when it needed to be. Merchants wanted the money to be spent between the harbor and Faneuil Hall. It truly was an independent community. All that had changed over the decades was the origin of the inhabitants. About 44% of the current residents were stabilized and of Italian descent. It had been a melting pot of immigrants for centuries.

An hour after we were settled into the condo, Graziano again begged us for some authentic pizza. By then, Susan and I were hungry as well and we decided to explore nearby streets for a small unassuming restaurant that could accommodate our palate.

We stopped by a local merchant and asked where we might find the *best* pizza. He mentioned only one restaurant that he preferred. It was Ernesto's on nearby Salem Street. Nodding our heads in agreement, we decided to give it a try. Oddly enough it was not far from Aldo Jr.'s Shoe Repair and a quick walk from Prince Street.

By late afternoon, the festive streetlights were illuminated for the holidays. Many sets were strung across Hanover and on Salem as well. Music could be heard everywhere, much of which emanated from tenements or from church steeple carillons. As dinnertime arrived, we easily found the recommended restaurant that would satisfy our cravings. In the window of Ernesto's was a sample menu with specials and a sign that read,

24 DIFFERENT SLICES—*For Here or To Go*

Inside, Susan was smiling and watching her son peruse the variety of pizza toppings. We were officially ingrained into the culture and it felt as if my old home were beckoning me to get reacquainted.

My train of thought was disrupted by the presence of the waiter at our table. His nametag said Giorgio and he was a young, handsome lad.

"Buona Sera." the waiter said, politely. I responded in turn, "Si . . . good evening" in return.

"May I take your order, Sir?" he asked. "Do you have any questions about the menu?"

We had already decided on a mushroom pizza, the larger one.

I ordered an Italian beer and Susan ordered a diet soda . . . she would have preferred a glass of Chianti Reserve. Her recent pregnancy awareness counteracted her desire for the red grape of choice—conventional wisdom prevailed.

After a few minutes, I felt like I'd never left the North End as a child. My thoughts were nostalgic and cathartic as I recollected many fun moments I had experienced during the years I had spent growing up here. It was one of the most comfortable moments in my life as an adult. *How had I stayed away so long?* The North End was my 'roots' and it clearly made me appreciate my life, family and the future reconnection to the Italian culture. My father had a profound influence on me, as a single parent. I was the biologic product of both of them, and yet he found solace in my 'creation' as a way to reconcile that his wife's DNA was still being carried on through me as a child. I had her eyes! That pleased him.

Chapter 25

Walking back to the condo after dinner, Susan felt a bit nauseated. She had experienced that feeling while carrying Graziano some nine years earlier. It was not the food, but the first trimester effects that often caused nausea. It waxed and waned and was generally worse in the morning.

Graziano noted a small plastic tree in the window of a store that had remained open in the early evening.

"Can we get that for Dad's old ornaments—ya know the old glass ones that he had as a boy?"

Susan was quick to respond and willed her malaise away.

"Sure, Honey. That'd look nice in your room with the old string of lights on it." The tree stood two feet tall with a wooden base for support. It would take a mere three minutes to put it together in the condo. That was something we could do as father and son while Susan rested on the couch. We purchased it without hesitation. The rest of the decorations, and the acquisition of a real 7-foot tree for the whole family, could be accomplished the next day, Christmas Eve afternoon. That would grace the living room.

Additionally, I would need to hang the 'Christmas Key' for Santa on Christmas Eve. I had fashioned the brass key with holly and a red bow. I noticed that a hook was still mounted on the right side of the doorframe of the condo entrance. It had been there all these years, coated in whatever color paint that owners had used when sprucing up the hallway.

There was much we needed to do the next day. Right now, we all needed to rest. We returned home and settled into the bedrooms, which we had prepared earlier with our linens and pillows.

"Buona notte," I said lovingly to my family. It meant, 'Good Night.' Graziano responded with a hug.

"Thanks for bringing us here, Dad," he offered, affectionately. He knew that I was pleased to be there. I was happy that he had learned the meaning of at least one Italian word, 'Grazie.' Coincidently, it was our affectionate nickname for him, his moniker for life.

Chapter 26

I couldn't sleep very well the first night in the condo, and lay back on the pillow with my arms folded behind my head. Susan was backed up to my body and sound asleep. She was in a peach-colored, silk nightgown, which I have given her the previous Christmas. Even in slumber she was a beauty to behold. I watched her breathe and it was obvious to me that she was contented, relaxed and perhaps in a deep dreamy mood. She lay still and now seemed undaunted by the transplantation to the North End for the holidays. If she was 'fazed' by the different plan this holiday, it was not obvious at this point.

I stared at her and knew exactly why we were married. We thought alike, had the same interests in general and adored our son. He was the *glue*, part of the love that held the family together. He completed the triangle. If we were to be blessed with a baby girl, that addition would add to an already solid family unit.

As I lie awake, I pondered the forthcoming Christmas events. I had already purchased presents that would be reflective of our weekend visit to the North End.

For Susan, I had bought more nightclothes from Victoria's Secret. They made her feel sexy. I also wanted her to have some jewelry therefore I had shopped at the noted Jeweler's Building on 333 Washington Street in Boston, during my last visit. There were deals to be had on gold and silver even though the price of gold was on the rise. Diamonds were discounted there since jewelers sold in volume and could pass on financial savings to the consumer. I purchased a necklace with a gold pendant of a mother and child. I had seen many versions of this piece but never one with a diamond embedded in the center of the charm. It was perfect for Christmas since it represented the Madonna and Child and poignant that Susan was pregnant with our second family member.

Uniquely, I wanted Graziano to have something that represented his heritage and I chose an historic Italian flag that I'd seen in an antique store adjacent to the North End. Eventually, he would be able to display it over his bed or hang it outside his window with a flag holder mounted on the window frame. We had seen others displayed that way during our walk on Hanover and Salem Streets. The unique flag was imported direct from Italy and was quite old.

From a common mast, the Italian flag is colored green, white and red, a rectangular piece with vertical stripes of color. A small 3" x 5" card that accompanied the flag gave a brief history of Italy's moniker. The green, in the eyes of historians, stood for—*hope,* the white,—*faith,* and the red,—*charity.* There were discrepancies over the meaning of the colors however. As the card suggested, the '*Tricolore*' represented the colors of the Civic Militia of Milan or the three *cardinal* virtues. The colors are even mentioned in Dante's, *Divine Comedy.*

Adopted in 1796 by the Lombard patriots in a French controlled area of Italy, the idea of 'tricolors' was implemented during the Napoleonic Wars. The Italian Republic in 1801 flew the flag, as well as the King of the Savoia dynasty, Carlos Alberto in 1848. At that time, it incorporated a cross and crown in the 'white' portion of the tricolors. Since 1945-46, the flag has been the official symbol of the Italian Republic; no symbolic emblem remains for any dynasty of the past.

In the end, it was clear from history that 'the French' had much to do with the style, the size of the rectangles and the colors that were selected as the Italian '*Tricolore.*' The flag that I purchased for Grazie was of a period in the late 1970s; supposedly the flag came from the region of Reggio Emilia—a geographical location that was the first area to actually formally 'adopt' the Italian flag.

I was to have another present for Graziano but could not present it to him until we returned home. I wanted desperately to replace the dog that he loved so dearly. Toward that effort, I was in touch with a breeder of the same type of dog as Rusty, who had died one year earlier. The reputable breeder had just what we wanted, but it would remain a post Christmas surprise until we returned to the Berkshires.

Eventually I must have dozed off for I knew morning would come all too fast and there would be much to do to make Christmas Eve and the following day of Christmas a success.

*   *   *

Friday morning I was up early making coffee. Before the family arose, I walked down to the pastry shop and bought some goodies to fuel the day. Twenty dollars later, I returned home to find Susan sitting at the kitchen table wrapping a present or two. She was already ahead of me—I would wrap any remaining gifts for them, later. I kissed her good morning and we talked about the day. I had already fashioned the Christmas Key (*Chiave*), complete with a sprig of holly and a red bow. I hid the gift for Graziano in the glove compartment of the car. That was already gift wrapped in advance to assure secrecy.

Grazie awoke and we ate breakfast kind of late. We still had to find a family tree but became preoccupied with placing a string of lights in his bedroom window, a fake wreath on his door and the small tree in his bedroom. It took some time to decorate the little tree on the dresser. I gave him the antique string of lights that I had as a child and the Christmas balls and ornaments that my father had saved for posterity. The box contained old metal tinsel in it as well. It was brittle and meshed, almost in a ball, but he still wanted to use it. We used everything we could to make it look like the days of old.

"That looks super, Dad," he offered, staring at the tree from a few steps back. He was still in pajamas and oddly had slept well the night before. Both Susan and I had worried that he might have nightmares and then awaken not knowing where he was. He fooled us by sleeping far better and longer than we did. I was still fatigued from my insomnia.

Both Susan and I were complimentary of the final tree project.

"Looks great, Son. Plug 'er in!"

Grazie managed to find an electrical outlet near the dresser. The string of lights responded with a glow that reflected off the glass ornaments like mirrors. They looked larger and actually magnified the colors of the lights, doubling the illumination almost as if a second string of lights had been added to the branches. It seemed a bit gaudy, but Grazie loved it.

"We have *one more* tree to decorate," I mentioned. Today, perhaps in an hour or so, we'll get the *big* one for the living room."

"Can't wait, Dad," he chimed. "Where'll we get it?"

"Down the street a bit," I said, "the bakery person said there were trees for sale not far from the Paul Revere house. That's not far away."

"How will we get it home?" he asked. "Car?"

"No," I responded, "we'll bring it home on your sled. I have it in the SUV." He had not seen it under the boxes and suitcases piled high for the weekend.

"We'll do like we do back home. Drag it on a sled—all the way to the house. There's enough snow on the sidewalks to handle the load."

"Cool," he said, with excitement "it'll be just like being back home."

"Do you miss *home* at Christmas?" Susan asked, with concern. That seemed to be her unnecessary angst for days.

"A bit," he said, "I miss the dog and I was thinking of Rusty." A tear or two appeared in his eyes. "Rusty is not with us this year."

"I know, Honey . . . we miss Rusty too, but I brought his picture with us just for you. He's here in spirit." Grazie managed a smile, a concerted effort under the sad circumstances. He placed the photo by the small tree. "I have the Christmas ball with his picture. That helps."

Susan changed the subject to help ameliorate the sad memories.

"Think Santa will bring you what you want tonight?"

"Sure . . . Santa always does," he said, confidently.

"Oh, really?" added Susan, teasing him.

"How do you know that?" she asked. "Have you been *that* good?"

"Sure," he replied, "I've been good for a long time and I'm doin' okay in school."

Susan reinforced his confidence.

"Yes, you've done well in school. "How about the cleaning of your room? Have you done that as often as I've asked?"

"Not exactly."

"Well . . . I would wonder then," she said, presenting him with a *reality* check.

I had to pipe in before he got worried.

"Well, Mom—he's helped with the snow shoveling and the cleaning up of the shed."

Susan nodded in agreement.

"True," she said.

She knew he seemed less worried after I spoke up to boost his spirits.

"I guess that helps Santa make his list of 'good things' you have done—longer, eh?"

"Yup."

Graziano was okay with the conversation and he regained his confidence. He seemed not to overestimate the positive side of his good fortune, actually appearing humble. After all, Santa was showing up tonight. He kept his comments positive for even *more* kudos.

"Guess so . . . hope so. He told me that he would come," he voiced, "at Quincy Market." Susan and I agreed that was good.

We managed to clean the kitchen, and everyone showered and dressed for the day's activities. I'd been in sweats all morning, including the trip for coffee and donuts. I needed to spruce up a bit before we left the condo. Because the chores were related to getting a tree, jeans seemed the best attire, including the consummate, Timberland boots. That way it would mimic the Western Massachusetts 'woodsy' look and the prior Christmas's that we were accustomed to. Grazie had his own pair of Timberlands.

Chapter 27

Elena had called us from her vacation spot down south and wanted to know how things were going. The whole LaFauci family seemed to be gathered there for Christmas. By the tone of her voice, she sounded relaxed and happy to be away from the cold and snow.

"You get in, okay?" she asked, with concern.

"Yes . . . no problem. Arrived late yesterday," I responded, confidently. "We're enjoying the condo."

"Good. I hope you have a fantastic weekend."

"We will. Already have a small tree up and about to get the 'big boy' next," I said, with exuberance. I was smiling from ear to ear.

"You sound very happy and I hope all of you have a nice time. Don't forget the events on the side streets. Walk around a bit. They will pop out at you. We'll finish the deal when I return. Right now, I'm heading for the beach." I chided her for teasing us.

"Merry Christmas to you and yours. Light a palm tree," I offered, joking. She responded in kind and told me it was near 80° F.

It seemed strange to chat with her so informally. We had just met a few weeks before and already we were becoming good friends. She was as happy for us as we were for her. It was one of her more pleasant real estate deals because the situation was unique. No one had ever had the opportunity to regain his or her old homestead in the North End—at least not in Elena's experience.

Following the call, I opened the alcove closet in the kitchen to retrieve our coats and noticed a box of tools that were 'the basics,'—a hammer, a wrench and pliers, nuts and bolts, a small saw and tape measure. The owners had left the bare essentials for routine electrical and plumbing repairs of which I'm sure there were many issues over the past few decades. The building was old and dated. Previous owners had 'jerry-rigged' pipes and electrical connections I'm sure, especially in the basement, where few people wanted to venture. The home inspector had recommended some minor changes for later, since the home basically met code. His appraisal was positive. He may have just wanted his $450 and was less stringent in his evaluation.

I grabbed the coats and two hangers fell on the floor as they always do. They seem to *mate* in the closet with the door closed—a common occurrence in the dark when no one is looking. In the process of bending over to retrieve them, I noticed a small metal door that was painted shut. I tapped on the ten inch square metal plate cover that seemed to be inoperable, obviously for decades or even years. It was hollow in sound. The plate was painted closed with the slots in the screw heads flat in appearance instead of revealing the indentation necessary for a screwdriver. The four screws held the plate to the wall. It appeared as if it was some sort of old electrical panel, with the box recessed, and the panel door flush to the wall. Two small hinges on the right side were coated with paint as well. There had once been a tab to open the door but the wire loop was missing.

I contemplated prying it open but Susan convinced me to address the unexpected odyssey later in the day. We were already late in acquiring the tree; that is if 'we were to have Santa place anything under it,' she had vocalized clearly.

*　　*　　*

Grazie was slow as usual, grabbing a Christmas toy of old and not paying much attention to our need to leave the warm, comfortable abode.

"Let's go, Son," I reminded him. Susan was already dressed in a parka, hat and gloves and was anxiously awaiting him to 'get a move on it.'

"It's a bit hot in here . . . can we get going?" she said, impatiently. "I've many things to do before dinner and we've yet to leave the house," she added, in short fashion.

Grazie was to blame. He was putting on his boots and fiddling with the laces that had come out of the eyelets of the leather. At this point we were losing our patience.

Suddenly, there was a crash in the hallway outside the condo door, the rumble of someone ascending the stairs like a drunken sailor. Susan and I were both startled. She was frightened and whispered cautiously,

"What *the hell* was that?" she asked, in a low voice.

"Don't know . . . don't open the door," I said, apprehensively.

Ten seconds later there was a knock on the door and heavy, exhaustive breathing. It was disconcerting to us and I was reluctant to approach the entrance. There wasn't a peephole to look out of or to see the intruder. Grazie was hiding by the refrigerator, a space too small for anything useful, except a small child.

"Dad?" he said, in fear. His eyes were wide with apprehension.

"It's okay," I whispered in his direction. I was the brave one and already heading for the closet since I noticed an old baseball bat tucked beneath the 'mating hangers.' I heard two voices conversing in a low whisper. I held the bat high like Griffey, Jr., circling it and slowly unlocked the chain.

"Nobody's home, I guess," one of them said, in a low voice. "Jeez," the other person voiced, apparently struggling, or in pain. "Knock again," said one of them, "maybe they're sleeping."

"This late in the day? Nah." He knocked again, harder.

There was a moment of silence. I finally had had it with the vagrants or daylight intruders. I grabbed the door handle with bat readied in hand and feet planted firmly.

"What the hell's goin' on?" I screamed, adrenaline rushing and my face flushed from anger.

"What the . . . ?" I yelled. Grazie at this point was close to crying.

"Merry Christmas and congrats!" Aldo, Jr., said, personally reeking of a bit of 'the vino' this early in the day. He smiled broadly as he held on to the lower end of a large balsam.

"Holy God," I added to the unexpected greetings, "What are you doing? I almost killed you," I reprimanded him.

"Jesus, Aldo," I continued while lowering the bat, "you scared the crap otta us! Merry Christmas, you crazy person! Let me help you there."

I grabbed on to a tree branch and helped him negotiate the corner of the doorway. There was no way to swing it around since the stairwell was narrow and limited.

"I thought I heard two voices," I said, expecting someone at the top end of the tree. I couldn't see beyond the base branches. They obliterated any view down the stairs or the sight of anyone else, if in fact someone was actually there.

"Kind of big," Aldo added, somewhat out of breath. "It wasn't *my* idea," he said, struggling to make the tree vertical and aligned with the doorway.

"Don't blame me."

I stood for a moment wondering what the heck he meant.

"Well, who the heck told you to do this?" I asked, in complete confusion, "The real estate gal?"

"Nope . . . some 'idiota' at da other end of the tree!"

I was at a loss for words until I got the tree centered and vertical. An enormous man stood on the stairs, totally bald and dressed like an older Italian merchant from the harbor.

"This guy told me to do this," added Aldo, smiling. "It's Dominick, your old friend."

I must say that tears appeared in my eyes at that very moment. "Dom? From the neighborhood?" I screamed, elated.

"Atsa me," he replied, entering the kitchen and releasing the tree while Aldo fought with the branches. We embraced and then shook hands.

"How in the hell . . . ?" I asked Aldo, hesitating. I repeated myself. "How in the hell did you find him?"

"It's a secret, but I knew that you guys used to get your Christmas trees together when you were young. Actually, I found him on the *ItaliNet*, the Internet," he volunteered. "He actually lives close by. My dad's not here today but *you two* are, so I told him you had moved *home*."

I stood back close-mouthed and grabbed Dom's shoulders shaking them gently but firmly, in awe of the fact that we had been reunited.

"This is awesome," I said, with total amazement at the serendipitous reunion. "This is Susan and my son, Graziano." They hugged and kissed cheeks, all except Grazie who found the ceremony unusual as a young lad.

"Pleasure to meet you," Susan added. "My husband has often spoken of you both, especially *this* guy, Dominick, who he had hoped to one day find again." She winked.

Susan and Grazie took off their coats, hats and boots as our son walked around the standing tree looking up at the top. "Wow," he commented, "it's a beauty!"

Aldo looked fatigued and we helped him steady the monster. The handsaw in the closet next to the toolbox would be needed for trimming, after all.

"Hope you have a stand for it," Aldo offered, with chagrin. He looked at Susan and Grazie for approval. They nodded and both reacted in unison by smiling.

"It's perfect!" I added.

"It's beautiful," offered Susan, smiling. "That's so nice of you. This is a special moment," she added. "Nothing could be more special than this get together," she repeated. "To see my husband so pleased, and happy to be with you, is all we could ask for this Christmas," she offered, shaking her head in disbelief.

"What's the chance of this happening to anyone?" she added. Everyone agreed it was like a miracle from above.

We laid the tree crossways in the foyer and the boys came into the kitchen for a while. Water drops trailed off the base of the tree, residual snow melt from the branches. It never lost a needle. It barely fit, even when laid at an angle, but the aroma of the pine immediately permeated the room after five minutes time. The *smell* was that of *Christmas*. I was at a profound loss of words and offered them a drink of something cheery and seasonal.

"Sit down, please," I told them, pointing my forefinger and extending my arm toward the kitchen chairs.

"Coffee, beer, wine, cola?" I asked, cordially.

"Wine would be in order," spoke Aldo. Dom agreed and all I could do then was stare at him—assimilating his features. I couldn't believe we were together again after numerous decades apart. Sadly, Aldo, Sr. was not alive. The redeeming factor was that we had his son to befriend and that was good enough for the holidays, *in absensia.*

"You lika da tree?" Aldo Jr. asked, with an augmented Italian accent. It was humorous.

"Are you serious? We love it . . . isa beauty," I said, mocking him. "We were just going out the door to find one and you guys showed up. How much do I owe you?"

"Nadda. Zero!" said Dominick. "We used to get our trees together, with our families. This is just a long overdue reunion and ongoing custom that we hopefully can repeat for many more years together."

"Agreed," I responded, smiling, "although . . . we *did* take a vacation from this custom for decades," I added, laughing. "Aldo, I don't know how you found Dom so easily." I commented, with amazement.

*　　*　　*

We spent the next hour catching up on old times. Dominick was married but had lost his wife, Julia, to breast cancer the year before. We were sad for him. He managed to continue his family line and had a daughter and a son in California. He retired from a job in Boston, one that involved the MBTA where he had spent thirty-five years working for one of the oldest public transport systems. It was the 'MTA' at one time and the subject of a song (*Charlie on the MTA*) that the Kingston Trio, a famous folk group, had recorded in the late 1950s.

Dom and Aldo had each brought an ornament for the tree, for Susan and Grazie. They had found a Santa and a porcelain Madonna and Child. The Madonna was hand-painted in Italy and they had purchased them from a local, North End store. Both Aldo and Dom were devout Catholics, even after many decades of changes in the Church and its issues. They stayed with the religion even after the scandals in Boston. Priests and bishops were still under the microscope for past grievances.

Susan excused herself to bake some cookies, this time from a 'commercial mix' while Dom, Aldo, Jr. and I caught up on old memories. We talked a lot about Aldo, Sr. and how we were the 'Three Musketeers' in our younger days, days that were carefree and pleasant most of the time. We agreed that growing up in 'Little Italy' provided us with experiences, culture and history that few kids today got to embrace. We could have chatted all afternoon but our family had much to do and Aldo needed to get back to his family. We agreed to never let these moments pass us by and to stay in touch by phone and email. We exchanged addresses and contact information as needed. Dom was now in the loop. The three of us were committed to staying in touch, especially in the forthcoming new year.

Both Aldo and Dom left a few minutes after they sampled the baked goods. We extended our Christmas wishes to them and to their families. It was tough to have them leave, especially after decades of being apart. Their kindness would be remembered forever.

Chapter 28

The living room tree went up in no time. We had found a tree stand in the cellar, one that was hung on a pegboard just waiting for someone to use it. Rusted and as old as it was, it worked well for the seven-foot balsam. I used the small handsaw to trim the bottom branches before we placed the tree in front of the window for all to see. Dragging the tree up the stairs had broken one or two branches. Within a half hour, it was drinking the water from the base of the stand. Grazie had heard that adding some sugar helped the tree live longer and better. We dissolved a tablespoon of sugar in warm water and he poured it into the well of the green and red metal stand.

The sets of lights went on quickly as both Grazie and I walked around the tree in circles, untangling the mess. We had hastily put the string sets away the previous year and more time was spent laughing and untangling the sets than applying the white mini-lights to the tree. Susan sipped alcohol-free wine on the couch until we had all the cords figured out. One or two additional sets were my dad's. They added color to the predominantly white bulbs.

"You ready for the ornaments yet, boys," she asked, with anticipation.

"Almost," I replied, fumbling with an extension cord or two as I tried to hide them from view under a homemade red felt tree skirt. Even without ornaments, the early afternoon dusk of winter made the room darker than normal. Buildings across the street that were once factories blocked the sun's rays.

"Ready, Dad?" Graziano said, wishfully.

"Sure, Son . . . plug it in."

In a moment of silence and anticipation, we watched as the tree illuminated brightly. One string was set to blink occasionally, just enough to enhance the beauty but not enough to deter from the hundreds of stationary white lights that brightened the whole room.

Susan hugged both of us, a group hug, and then she opened one of three boxes of ornaments that we had brought from our home in Washington.

"Hang them one at a time," she ordered, gently. "Some are old and fragile."

We boys were obligated to get her permission as to where they looked best. Grazie had free liberty to put anything anywhere but I was sure that mother would move a few to another location after he was in bed for the night.

"Put the larger ones on the lower branches," she instructed. "The small ones go up top." We followed her lead.

"What about the tree top? Do we have something for the top, Dad?"

"Just the star-like ornament from last year," I suggested. "It's in the boxes somewhere. We can add it last."

Once we were done, we sat on the living room couch together. We admired the gorgeous glow that emanated from the unexpected gift from Aldo, Jr., and Dominick.

*   *   *

Hunger pangs set in and we needed to think about dinner. We unplugged the tree for safety and dressed for the cold outside. Looking out the front windows, we saw that it was lightly snowing. We could hear music playing; the holiday spirit had already begun. It was nearly the night before Christmas. Christmas Eve dinner would be at a local restaurant. Susan had already baked cookies and made hot chocolate for later.

The restaurant, *Bella Pesce* satisfied our desires. The menu in the window had a nice variety of fish, pork, veal and pasta dishes to appease anyone. It was quaint and charming with seasonal red tablecloths and Italian music playing low in the background for ambiance. We were early so there were few people out and about—Italians like to eat later, in a more formal setting. Many were probably off to early Mass or other religious services.

We hoped to peek into the foyer and sanctuary of St. Leonard's before returning home. Often, Catholic churches were decorated with garlands and flowers, poinsettias and white and red carnations. The altars would surely be covered with bouquets and arrangements donated by parishioners.

We relaxed at dinner and then left for St. Leonard's. After the church visit, we walked past a few side streets near the harbor to see the lights. We headed home to Prince Street and our comfortable escape for the holiday weekend. It was 7 P.M. and we were hoping to have Graziano in bed by 9. There were still a few things left to do before Santa arrived.

Chapter 29

"Dad, what about the special key for Santa?" our son asked. I had almost forgotten about the one in the glove compartment.

"I will see if I can find one," I appeased him, momentarily. I made believe that I was looking in the boxes, the ones we had brought from home.

"Not here," I concluded. "Perhaps it's in the car. I'll check."

Grazie's eyes opened wide when he saw the shiny brass key, holly and red ribbon. He had no idea that there was really a 'key' for kids whose homes had no chimneys or fireplaces for Santa to descend. His eyes were like saucers as he held the ribbon high in the air. The heavy key swung gently back and forth.

"Where will we put it?" he asked, impatiently.

"Let me show you, Son," I replied. We walked to the door and I showed him the piece of bent metal on the door jam. The odd fashioned hook appeared to be an old nail that was firmly embedded in the wood. It was coated with a multitude of colored paint layers. No one had bothered to remove it, even after all these years. It had a square head at the top, which suggested that it was very old and possibly handmade or forged.

"Can we put it up now?" he asked.

"Let's wait until you go to bed," I offered. "That way it will be the last thing we do before we go to sleep. Does that sound fair?"

"Okay . . . I can wait."

One thing for sure, our son was always conciliatory and flexible. He was the best kid and we were proud of him. I reassured him that Santa would find the key.

Susan called me into the living room. She had noticed that the lights on the tree had flickered and she was concerned. Some of the light sets were old and the tree fresh. We didn't need a fire. I inspected the sets visually and then the wall socket. Although the condo had been upgraded, there was nothing to suggest from the home inspection that any of the wiring was not up to code. What was in fact visible, met code. There was no way for the inspector to know what was behind the walls. The inspector asserted that he had checked everything to Boston code standards.

"I'll look around the condo for an electrical panel," I said, immediately perusing the closets and alcoves in the bedroom and living room.

I asked Susan to check the light sets for a loose bulb. That might make the whole set flicker if one bulb was not firmly tightened in an older set.

I remembered the metal plate in the kitchen closet where the box of tools was stored—the panel that was painted shut and original to the home when I was a child. I had noticed it earlier and it might be an old electrical fuse box worth investigating.

In the early days, there were fuses, which were 15 or 20 amps, and when they 'blew,' my father would stick a copper penny in the receptacle to keep the circuit going. Copper was conductive and pennies were copper. It was an unsafe practice, but one to tie him over until he bought a replacement fuse. Everyone used the quick-fix alternative. Circuit breakers finally emerged many years later. When they were faulty, they would make a rattling sound.

On a makeshift shelf in the closet was a flashlight, which came in handy. Shining it on the painted door of the box, I again noticed the four screws that held the plate secure. I was not able to easily free them up. The cover almost seemed soldered shut from paint. A screwdriver from the toolbox made it easy to scrape the screw heads clean of existing paint. A single groove appeared in each screw head, a groove that a flathead screwdriver could finally fit into easily. The metal screws were more like wood screws than machine screws, which often had rounded tops. I ran the screwdriver blade around the outside edge of the metal panel to loosen it. The paint was layers thick and cream-colored, basically the *latest* color of the inside of the closet. Once the screws were removed, the plate remained stuck. I gently pried the faceplate loose.

I was shell-shocked to see what was behind the metal cover. The metal box contained two rumpled pieces of tissue paper that had been rolled and folded separately and contained some objects. One was large and the other one was smaller. There were no electrical connections, fuses, or mechanical parts typical of a fuse box. The metal box was recessed by some eight inches in depth.

"Susan!" I yelled, in haste and confusion. "Come here . . . please. Look!"

I backed out of the closet touching nothing. She approached the closet door and asked, "What's wrong?" Graziano came into the kitchen and stood silent in the confusion.

"Look at this!" I said, pointing to the recessed metal box and contents. She peered into the void and looked puzzled.

"What's in there?"

"I don't know. Grab the papers and hand them to me gently—here in the kitchen light. Let's see what the heck we have."

She carefully took out the two tissue-covered items and handed them to me one at a time. They weren't heavy, yet the opaqueness of the tissue hid the contents. I walked to the kitchen table and laid them down. She turned on the table lamp.

"What is it Dad—a *skeleton?*" Grazie asked, with fear.

"No, Son. There's no skeleton. I don't know what they are. Let's investigate. Whatever it is in there, they've been there a long time."

"Open them, Dad. Please open them."

Susan reached in one more time and found an envelope that accompanied the objects. The paper was old and it contained a note that was still sealed inside. She handed me the envelope and we sat at the table together. The envelope read,

To whoever finds these items, please read the note inside.

The outside of the envelope was written in English, and again in Italian. I sat silently holding the envelope up to the light. It was discolored over time but not as discolored as one would see from something exposed to sunlight. This had been kept in the dark for many years.

As Grazie grew impatient, I gently opened the sealed envelope and tears came to my eyes. Susan reacted immediately. "What is it, Hon . . . what's it say?"

I handed her the note and wiped my eyes with the back of my hands, one at a time. That didn't stop the flow of tears.

"What is it, Dad—bad news?"

"No, Son. It's not bad news, it's good news."

"Why are you crying Dad, if it's good news?" he asked. It was a good question from an astute young boy who was now sympathetically sad himself.

Susan hugged me without saying a word. She was emotional. Her eyes glistened and she sought out a nearby Kleenex tissue. She had read the note and whispered to Grazie. The folded note was also in both languages.

I focused on the packages of tissue paper and asked Graziano to open the smaller one of the two. He was hesitant knowing that we were emotional. We smiled to dispel his concern. He had no clue what was in the packages.

"It's a *key*! A *Christmas* Key! A *Chiave*, Dad!"

"Yes, Son," I laughed, "that's what it is . . . an old Santa key," I said, hugging him closely. Susan joined in.

"It was mine when *I* was a child," I confirmed. "Do you understand that, Son? It's almost as old as me," I said, laughing. He nodded in agreement.

"*That* key was the one I thought was lost," I voiced, emotionally. "My father placed it in the sealed box before he moved to the western part of Massachusetts, and out of this house in the North End. It's amazing that it's still here."

All Grazie could say was, "Wow. It's not shiny like mine and the ribbon is faded and smelly," he said, holding the item near his nose. Susan and I laughed, overcompensating for the tears of joy.

I held on to the key and studied it. Grazie gently opened the other tissue package. It was just as amazing. In it, was a small Polaroid picture of my mother and father, and the 'angel' of my youth—the Christmas tree angel that adorned our tree when I was a youngster. A small tag attached to the angel read,

For my child, son or daughter,
Love, Mother

It was obviously a gift from my mother directed to her forthcoming birth child, a child she would never get to know due to her morbidity during labor and death *post partum*. That child was *me* in her womb, the Christmas before my birth. She was planning to give me the 'angel' to place on the tree each year. The note from my father explained her intentions and the relevance of the Santa Key—the '*Christmas Chiave*' as he referred to it in the note.

*　　*　　*

We were exhausted from the unexpected but welcomed encounter from the past, two gifts that made this Christmas even more special. No one would have known that the items were in the wall. Apparently no one needed to open the panel in the past. It sat silent, seemingly awaiting my unanticipated acquisition of the condo. It was fate, not chance, akin to the finding the Titanic after seventy plus years of mystery and numerous sub oceanic efforts.

The bulbs on the tree probably had flickered because one bulb was indeed loose. I like to think that someone was guiding me to the closet—a spiritual destiny. *St. Anthony perhaps?* Susan managed to find the bad bulb, by trial and error.

Was that a message from my father? Did he 'will me' into that closet? Or, was it my mother by his side saying, 'This is now for Graziano.' It didn't matter what the reason was. We could only guess.

Chapter 30

Prior to retiring to bed, Graziano had replaced the glass star on the top of the tree with the 'angel' ornament. I held him high in order to reach the point of the balsam. He put the star on his own little tree in his bedroom.

We hung both of the '*Christmas Keys*' on the front door hook. First was Grazie's, then mine. They looked great together (the old and the new) and doubled our chances for Santa to be kind to us.

"Mom, you don't have one," he said, sadly. "How will Santa find you tonight and bring you presents?"

Susan hugged our son closely. She was speechless for a moment. Graziano was always 'about others.'

"He already found me," she offered, with love. "Santa Claus and God brought me *you* . . . and *your father.* I have all I need, right here."

The stockings we laid out on a wing chair near the tree. A Nativity scene, the one of my youth, was on a nearby table. Grazie placed baby Jesus in the manger and we retired to the bedroom. We managed to go to bed by 9 P.M. All three of us slept in the same bed Christmas Eve.

Epilogue

Christmas Day came fast. Grazie awoke at 5 A.M. and first checked where 'the keys' were on the hook outside the door.

"They're gone, Dad," he said, alarmed. "They're not here."

"Check inside the kitchen, perhaps," I offered, smiling, while wiping my eyes of sleep.

They were no longer missing. He looked on the kitchen table and saw them lying beside a plate of half-eaten cookies and a partial glass of milk. The milk was nearly gone. The carrots for the reindeer were missing . . . all but one or two orange remnants remained as evidence of the reindeers' teeth.

We saw that Santa had indeed arrived and that the big tree had many presents under it. We lit all the lights on both trees and sat nearby with coffee and hot cocoa, in hand.

The angel on top of the tree was as beautiful in the morning as it was at night. The golden outfit and white halo and intricate wings were radiant. Looking at her features, it was as if I was a *child* again.

Susan gave me the book about the North End history and I gave her the jewelry and an assortment of summer clothes that she had desired. JC Penny and Victoria's Secret had come through again. She loved the Madonna and Child pendant and wore it that morning.

Graziano made out like a bandit. The Italian flag was a hit and he hung it from the window sash. He received toys and clothes, basic clothes that he was less enamored with than the toys. There were children's books and a 'special' Santa note that told him that he had a surprise waiting for him back home in Washington. Santa claimed that it was 'special delivery' and he'd have to sign for it. I didn't divulge the gift but told him it was probably something fuzzy—something that he had always wanted.

"Is it a horse, Dad . . . or a stuffed animal?"

"Ya never know, Son . . . bears can be fuzzy!" I teased.

"No! Not a bear! . . . a *bear*?" he repeated.

You'll have to wait and see," I said, firmly.

After Christmas we drove home to the Berkshires. We had a wonderful time in the North End, enjoyed Christmas Mass at St. Leonard's, cooked a Christmas dinner and then drove west when it was almost dark.

In time, the condo would be ours for good. We left it as we had found it, clean and simple as if no one had been there. We repacked the ornaments and took down the beautiful tree as quickly as we had put it up. The *Christmas Chiave* and the 'angel' were specially packed to avoid breakage. They would have their place at all future Christmases.

Graziano was now the proud owner of both keys and the 'angel.' They would remain with him forever, including the condo, when he and his sibling were older. That would be many years into the future, Susan and I hoped. Grazie's own life with his family and his own children would each need a *Christmas Chiave* and an 'angel' of their own.

As we were driving home with our son asleep in the back seat, I knew that a dog breeder of 'Goldens' was shipping a puppy, Rusty II to Graziano, and to our Washington abode. It was, after all, the most incredible Christmas of my life and hopefully for my family as well. My laptop was awaiting my fingers, and I promised myself to pen this very story in every detail.

May everyone give their loved ones two things on December 25th: a *Christmas Chiave* and a special 'angel' for the treetop . . .

Oh . . . and my book!
Buon Natale / Merry Christmas to all!

P.S. Smitty left a message on the home answering machine. He wanted to chat about a potential screenplay of one of my books. He had actually read one.

Acknowledgements

*I wish to extend my appreciation and thanks to my wife, Brenda,
for her conscientious review of the manuscript and invaluable input in
the edit and production of the novel. Her 'eagle eyes' caught many
a faux pas, typo and breach of continuity. Thank you also to my
brother, Tony and to my colleague/ grad school mentor,
Donald L. Black, Ph.D. for reviewing the manuscript.*

*I also wish to express my loving thanks to my direct and indirect
relatives of Italian and Italian-American descent, many of whom
were the inspirational catalyst for this Christmas tale.*

Cover photo: *by the author, JPP © 2008*

Back cover author photo: *choreography and photography by
Stephanie Lynn Polidoro © 2008—a budding artisan in her own right at age 13*

Additional books by the author, J. P. Polidoro, Ph.D.

Available from bookstores (special order), Amazon.com, Longtailpublishing.com, Xlibris.com, BN.com, and from Ingram Books

* *Rapid Descent—Disaster in Boston Harbor,* 2000
ISBN# 0-9677619-0-5

* *Project Samuel—The Quest for the Centennial Nobel Prize,* 2001
ISBN# 0-9677619-1-3

* *Return to Raby—A New England Novel,* 2003
ISBN# 0-9677619-2-1

Sniff—A Novel, 2004, Xlibris
ISBN# 1-4134-6558-7

Lavatory 101—A Bathroom Book of Knowledge. 2004, Xlibris
ISBN# 1-4134-8374-7—a book of trivia

Brain Freeze—321° F—Saving Reggie Sanford, 2005, Xlibris
ISBN# 1-4134-9768-3

Tattoo—Incident at the Weirs, 2007, Xlibris
ISBN# 978-1-4257-7680-0

---

*Longtail Publishing, 176 Pleasant Street, Laconia, NH 03246

www.longtailpublishing.com

LaVergne, TN USA
31 December 2009
168675LV00001B/105/P